I0451452

BEDDING
the Boss

Bedding The Bachelors Book 8

by
VIRNA DEPAUL

Bedding the Boss
Copyright © 2017 by Virna DePaul

All rights reserved. Without limiting the rights under copyright reserved above, no part of this publication may be reproduced, stored in or introduced into a retrieval system, or transmitted, in any form, or by any means (electronic, mechanical, photocopying, recording, or otherwise) without the prior written permission of the copyright owner.

This is a work of fiction. Names, characters, places, brands, media, and incidents are either the product of the author's imagination or are used fictitiously.

License Notes
This e-book is licensed for your personal enjoyment only. This e-book may not be re-sold or given away to other people. If you would like to share this book with another person, please purchase an additional copy for each person you share it with. If you're reading this book and did not purchase it, or it was not purchased for your use only, then please purchase your own copy. Thank you for respecting the author's work.

BEDDING THE BOSS

After discovering his fiancée was in love with his best friend, wealthy Eric Davenport left Los Angeles to return to his small-town roots. A year later, he's opening a ranch and love is the last thing on his mind.

Lexi Fischer's a rodeo baby who fell in love with movies in the back of her father's R.V. She's driving across country, working odd jobs to make it to LA and fulfill her dream of becoming a screenwriter.

When Lexi meets Eric, he's a confusing combination of earthy and sophisticated. They were only supposed to have one night, but then Eric makes Lexi an offer tough to refuse: work for him for the summer and he'll make sure she gets to LA, promising he'll keep his hands to himself.

Unable to resist, Lexi agrees. But as the summer progresses, feelings between Lexi and her boss spiral out of control. Can Eric survive loving another woman destined to leave him? And will Lexi realize that love won't interfere with her dreams but rather make all her dreams come true?

PROLOGUE

On the eve of his wedding to Brianne Whitcomb, Eric Davenport sat next to the bed where his fiancée lay, waiting for the sound that could mean the end of his life as he knew it, or at least, the end of his life with Brianne.

As vice-president of the company that had made his father a multi-millionaire before he was forty, Eric had been blessed with a privileged upbringing and the knowledge he'd always have a place in his father's business. He'd known how lucky he was and enjoyed life to the fullest. But lately he'd been restless. Dissatisfied. And his general dissatisfaction had started to spill over into everything: work, home, even his relationship with Brianne. He'd sensed the same dissatisfaction in her, but chalked it up to stress, telling himself once the wedding was over, things would get back to normal.

Then a week ago, he'd discovered the truth.

God, Brianne, what a mess we've gotten ourselves into, he thought.

Brianne was fast asleep, clearly exhausted from visiting with friends and family at the rehearsal dinner earlier that night, not to mention all the work that went into planning a high society wedding. Even if she hadn't been an event planner, Brianne's perfectionism and sense of aesthetic would have made planning the wedding a difficult task, but add in her chosen profession, and she'd been determined to throw an event people would talk about for years.

The funny thing was, despite her ties to high society, Brianne was one of the most down-to-earth, sweet, and kind women in the world, not to mention drop-dead gorgeous with a body made for sin. It was no wonder he'd jumped at the chance to date her when it presented itself, and what had followed had been six terrific years.

Only now he suspected they'd been fooling themselves. Now he wondered if the fact the whole world viewed them as the perfect couple—the man and woman who came from similar backgrounds, shared similar interests, and never fought—had somehow disguised the fact they were actually better suited as friends than lovers.

Now he was playing devil's advocate, disregarding all the reasons that he and Brianne belonged together, and focusing on the reasons that indicated that might not be true.

One very big reason specifically.

He wished he didn't have to. That he could dismiss his concerns as typical wedding jitters. He wished he could climb into bed with Brianne right now.

Take her in his arms.

Tell her how much he loved her.

Tell her how excited he was to be exchanging vows with her the next day in front of all their family and friends.

It was what he should be doing. How he should be feeling.

He'd wanted to spend the rest of his life with her. But that was when he'd convinced himself she felt the same way.

Instead, Eric was probably going to have to do something that his family and friends weren't going to understand, something that could in all likelihood make Brianne hate him—at least at first. Though to be fair, he told himself, if he called off the wedding it probably wouldn't come as a complete surprise to Brianne. She'd sensed something was off between them as well. Earlier, she'd even questioned whether *Eric* was having second thoughts.

What she didn't talk about was the reasons *she* might be having second thoughts.

In that moment, as if she could read his mind, Brianne stirred, stretching her arms and legs out, and smiling in a way he'd never actually seen before. Then she sighed. The sound was breathy and sexual. Her hand rose, cupping her breast, and she massaged the lush mound, giving away the intensity of her dream even before she moaned.

Eric closed his eyes and listened to the words that spilled from her lush lips.

She said she wanted him. She said she needed him.
Only the name she spoke wasn't Eric's.
It was Eric's best friend's name.
Gabe.

1

One year later
Buffalo Falls, Montana

Eric had sampled 60-year-old bourbons. French wines. Saki from a monastery in Japan. Twenty thousand dollar bottles of champagne. But as he watched the golden bubbles rise in his glass and took a hearty sip, he had to admit that Budweiser on tap was the drink of the gods. Tilting his baseball cap up off his forehead, he took another sip, letting the stress of the day roll off his back like water in a shower.

"Save some for the fishes, Eric," Jacob said as he clapped Eric on the back and sat on the barstool next to him. Jacob Tedesco and his brother Dean had been Eric's friends since they were in diapers. They'd spent almost every summer of their childhoods skipping rocks and talking about girls on the riverbanks a mile from the very bar they sat in. Although they'd kept in touch over the years, the friendship between Eric and Jacob had grown even stronger since Eric had moved to Buffalo Falls last year, leaving behind his home in L.A., not to mention his family, his business, his fiancée, and his best friends, all in one fell swoop.

Talk about starting over from scratch.

"Fishes don't drink beer, Jake," Eric replied, even as he realized that thinking of his old life hadn't filled him with the pain it once had.

And it hadn't for quite a while now.

Thank God.

So yes, it turned out Brianne had loved Gabe even when she'd been with Eric—even when they'd been engaged. And yes, her refusal to admit her feelings for Gabe even to herself had compelled Eric to take serious action and leave behind his life in California. But in the end, the two people he'd loved most had finally made it where they belonged: each other's arms. And now Eric was where *he* belonged. Montana had been his new beginning. It was now his future.

"Do all billionaires state the obvious like that?" his friend Dylan Quinn asked as he took the bar stool on the other side of Eric. He signaled the bartender for a beer. "In that case, sign me up. Doesn't sound so hard."

The bartender, Marina Howell—also someone Eric had known practically since infancy—quickly brought beers for Jacob and Dylan. She set them down carefully, like she was terrified of spilling even a drop. She had a big smile for Jacob and Eric, but dropped her eyes away from

Dylan even as her cheeks heated to an alluring peach.

"You want another, Eric?"

"I'm doing fine for now, Marina," he said, automatically using the quiet voice that most people used with her. There'd always been something delicate about her, something besides her lean frame, that gave the impression a strong wind could toss her right over. And that was even before what had happened to her five years ago.

Once again, Eric told himself how truly lucky he was in spite of the events of last year. Marina had had to deal with so much more. So had Dean, Jacob's brother, for that matter. The sole survivor in a horrific plane crash, Dean had dealt with the tragedy by leaving everything behind to drive trucks in the Alaskan wilderness. Jacob said he was doing fine, but Eric knew Dean's family worried about him. Even Jacob and Dylan had their shit to deal with. They all did. Eric was just lucky that, with his money, he could move on from his troubles easier than most. He certainly wasn't going to forget that anytime soon. No more wasting time. He had a dream to fulfill and he was finally doing it.

The second Marina was out of earshot, both Jacob and Eric turned to stare at Dylan.

"Now what, pray-tell, was that all about?" Jacob asked Dylan, fluttering his eyelashes like a southern debutante.

"What?" Dylan asked, frowning into his beer. But his eyes flicked over to Marina for just a split second.

"I think what Jake wants to know is why Marina Howell started blushing like a Georgia peach the second she got within ten feet of you," Eric said. Dylan met his gaze, initiating a stare-down that he was destined to lose. Eric hadn't helped turn his father's business into a billion-dollar enterprise by backing down to anyone.

Though that tenacity hadn't exactly helped with your engagement to Brianne, had it?

Shit. So he wasn't as over it as much as he'd thought.

No matter.

With the ease of practice, Eric shoved away thoughts of Brianne and their broken engagement, and instead focused on the fact that Dylan had indeed glanced away first.

"Who's to say why women do anything," Dylan said. "They're a fucking mystery."

"That sounds a lot like the bitter musings of a rejected man," Jake said, clinking his glass against Eric's.

"Yeah, well, you two would know about rejection better than anyone," Dylan shot back. As soon as the words were out of his mouth, Dylan's eyes widened and darted to Eric. "Shit, I didn't mean that, Eric. I was talking about Jake here. Of course Brianne didn't reject you. I mean, you rejected her first and—"

Eric forced a smile and waved his hand. God, would he ever be able to dodge his past? No, not when everyone in this town knew what had happened. "I knew what you meant, Dylan. Now stop stalling and tell us about Marina."

Dylan stared at him for several more seconds, then

finally relaxed and said, "Told you, nothing to tell. Now can we drop it and enjoy our beers and focus on that table of ladies that are looking our way."

Slyly, first Jake then Eric zeroed in on the table of four beautiful women that were indeed looking their way. They didn't look familiar, weren't locals to Buffalo Falls, and for a moment, Eric wondered what they saw. One thing was certain: they didn't look at Eric in his jeans and button-down shirt and think he was a billionaire tycoon who just last year had taken over running his grandparents' hardware store.

Jesus, even he knew how ridiculous *that* one sounded.

Even so, he'd been enjoying running the store. More recently, he'd been enjoying focusing on a new project: starting up his very own ranch. Unfortunately, he didn't have time to do both. He needed to find some full-time help for his grandparents' store, which he'd promised to look after while his grandparents went off to see the world. All the times he'd offered to pay for a first class trip around the world for them, they'd turned him down. And now they'd scrimped and saved for damn near fifteen years to take a third rate trip across Europe. They were in hog heaven. Emailing him adorable, lengthy updates filled with blurry selfies.

Jake took his hat off, tossed it on the bar and stood up. "Speaking of women, let's see if I can rustle us up a few." He sauntered over to pick out something on the juke box. Eric watched him go and had to admit that when it came to picking out the right song at the right moment,

Jacob Tedesco had a sixth sense.

With Jake leaning over the juke box, combing through the singles, Eric gestured in Marina's direction. "So, what happened?"

"Nothing, man," Dylan replied, his dark eyes following the movements of Marina's hands as she dried a few glasses and hung them on hooks over the bar. He hesitated, then kept going. "Nothing that hasn't happened a hundred times before."

Eric looked back and forth between Dylan and Marina, intrigued. A hundred times before? What was that supposed to mean? He opened his mouth to ask but felt a hand clap down on his back.

"Eric, what's good at the old O'Rourke ranch?" Will Owens asked as he signaled for a beer from Marina. Owens was another friend from childhood, not quite as close to Eric as Dylan or Jacob, but still a good guy. With his blonde hair and bright blue eyes, kids used to call him Ken Doll, until he'd beat the shit out of them.

Eric thought of the dilapidated ranch that was, even now, calling his name. Telling him to get started. "Good," he said. "She needs a ton of work, but she's got the makings of something amazing."

"Sure enough," Will said, accepting his beer from Marina with a wink and healthy tip. She flashed him a smile and then scurried back to the other end of the bar. "You need any help in that arena?"

Will owned a successful ranch himself. Ranching was in his family's blood. He could have been salty that Eric was starting his own so close to where Will's was, but instead here Will was, generously offering to help him out.

"You really mean that, don't you?" Eric said to Will.

Will nodded. "Of course, man. I'm well aware of the satisfaction that running a successful ranch can bring. I want that for my friend." He clapped Eric on the back again. "However, seeing as you're one rich bitch, I couldn't give a flying fuck whether or not your ranch turns a profit."

Jacob gave his signature hooting laugh as he came back to join his buddies, the first strains of 'Chain of Fools' rolling out over the bar. The women at the table were looking at them again, and Eric noticed a few other women poking their heads up like prairie dogs, starting to sway to the tune of the song.

He hadn't even noticed them in the bar before the song had come on. He shook his head. Jacob certainly had a gift.

"Ain't that the truth. That reminds me, drinks are on you tonight, Eric," Jake said, planting himself back on his barstool but swiveling around for a good look at the women who'd moved to the dance floor. Surveying his dirty work.

"You'll pay for your own damn drink, Tedesco," Dylan growled, face sour enough to scare Medusa off. "Just because Eric's got money doesn't mean he needs to float your ass every night of the week."

"What's a couple of beers between friends?" Jake asked, holding his hands up in mock surrender.

"I'll tell you what," Eric said to the group. "Drinks are on me if Jake can do something amazing. Give us a little entertainment."

"Oh boy," Dylan grumbled, sucking down the rest of his beer and signaling Marina for another one.

"What kind of entertainment?" Jake asked, obviously up for anything.

"You gotta get a woman to leave this bar with you in under fifteen minutes," Will interjected, getting in on the fun as well.

"I thought you said you needed me to do something amazing?" Jake blustered. "That's just a typical Friday night."

Jake stood and executed a runner's stretch, cracking his knuckles and making all the men laugh and roll their eyes. Jake flipped around to face the men and started moonwalking his way toward a group of women on the dance floor.

"Oh, lord," Marina said as she set Dylan's beer in front of him. "Who's he got his eye on now?"

Dylan immediately turned to her. Eric noticed that Dylan's hand curled, momentarily, over Marina's on his glass. She jumped back as if she'd been burned. She licked her lips and dropped her eyes.

"You know he's got his eye on everyone and anyone," Dylan said, his voice light despite the intensity of the moment that had just passed between them.

Marina cleared her throat and lifted her eyes again. But she looked at Eric and Will, not at Dylan. "He should've gone for the brunette down at the end of the bar; she's been stuck talking to Ray Fogerty for twenty minutes." Marina tossed her thumb toward the end of the bar before disappearing back toward the kitchen.

Eric looked over to where Marina had gestured, and sure enough, there was Ray. Obnoxious ass hat Ray Fogerty talking some woman's ear off.

She was turned away so Eric couldn't see her face. She wore a thin gray tank top and jeans. Her honey blonde hair tumbled over one pretty little shoulder and down toward her elbow. She leaned the side of her head onto her hand and Eric could see the glitter of a ring on each of her fingers. As if she could suddenly sense the gaze of the other men, the woman's shoulders tightened. She tossed the hair back from her face and looked over her shoulder. Her dark eyes immediately found Eric's.

Ho.

Ly.

Shit.

The heat from her stare raced all the way through his body like an electric shock. Every single part of him just stood up and took notice. Including one part that was extremely hard to ignore. Eric shifted on his barstool in the hope it would loosen his suddenly tight pants a little. No dice.

The woman quickly turned back around and Eric could see a lovely little flush working its way over her neck and shoulders. He wanted to taste that flush. Chase it as it bloomed over her skin with his teeth and tongue.

When he heard Will let out a low whistle behind him, Eric bristled. No. Hell no.

"Mine," Eric said, just seconds before Will did.

"What the fuck, Quick Draw?" Will grumbled.

"Beat it, Owens," Eric said to his friend as he finished off the last of his beer. It had been

over a year since he'd moved to Montana. Over a year since he'd been engaged to Brianne.

Over a year since he'd felt a strong attraction to any woman. At least, nothing like he was feeling now.

His night had just gotten a lot more interesting.

* * *

Breathe, Lexi, breathe. YOGA BREATHS!!!! Although Lexi suspected that yoga breaths weren't nearly as useful when you were internally screaming at yourself about them.

But she could still feel the ice blue stare of the man across the bar. The skin all over her body tightened in a completely delicious way because she knew he was still watching her. She could feel it. What a flipping hottie. The kind of hot that made the music fade away. Chestnut brown hair, carved face, confident stare. The kind of stare that says, *oh you wore panties? Cute that you thought you'd need them.*

"And remember that part where he's leaning out the car with that machine gun, like 'yaaaaaaaaaaaah'," the cowboy sitting next to her said as he pretended to shoot a gun into the air. Lexi commanded herself to start paying attention to him again. What was his name? Roy? Rick? Ray? Whatever it was, he was perfectly nice, kinda cute. And she'd been having a semi nice time talking to him. Well, except for the fact that he'd been yammering on about the same action movie—one she'd repeatedly reminded him that she hadn't seen—for the last fifteen minutes.

Lexi shifted in her seat and tried to ignore the shock of electricity that rolled through her body when she thought about Mystery Man's blue eyes. She had a perfectly good man in front of her and she was being rude. Even if he was being kind of rude himself, jabbering on about something that she obviously didn't care about.

"I'm more of an old-school movie type of girl, myself," she told him, taking a sip of her whiskey neat.

"Oh, you mean like Diehard?" he asked, lighting up like a kid on Christmas.

Lexi, on the other hand, dimmed like a light bulb after somebody turned on a hairdryer. "No. No not really. I meant more like Casablanca. Breakfast at Tiffany's. To Kill a Mockingbird. Planet of the Apes…" Lexi trailed off, her voice becoming more and more astonished as each movie she named garnered exactly zero evidence of recognition from him.

"Yeah," he said, scratching a hand over his smooth chin. "I think my mom likes some of those movies."

God Almighty. It took everything Lexi had not to roll her eyes at this schmuck. Come on. She was a reasonably hot girl, right? Sure, she dressed a little tomboy and she never wore makeup or did anything to her hair besides wash it, but she had all the right girl parts. She certainly had enough boobs and ass to at least warrant a blip of effort from this guy. She was *at least* hot enough to not get compared to his mom.

This conversation was going down hill fast. Lexi hadn't cried her eyes out after having to sell her horse— even if Maple's new home looked like an equine's dream come true—only to drag her ass out to a bar to have the latest Bourne movie reenacted by a guy who'd ordered a plate of fries and hadn't offered her any. She'd come to the bar to… well, she wasn't really sure of the answer to that.

Drown her sorrows? Maybe. She was going to miss Maple so much. A beautiful black and white paint, Maple had a mane like silk and eyes that would break your heart. Eyes the memory of which *did* break Lexi's heart as she stared into her drink and tuned out the Matt Damon enthusiast sitting next to her.

Money sucked. No. Strike that. Money fucking sucked. If money didn't exist, then she wouldn't have had to sell the sweetest creature on earth that morning just to make ends meet. Lexi swallowed down the rest of her whiskey before she realized that if money didn't exist, she wouldn't have been able to buy Maple in the first place. Aaand now she was just confusing herself.

"Are you even listening to me?" Ron/Roy/Ricky asked her in an irritated voice, bringing Lexi out of her Maple-related cloud of depression.

"What? Oh. I'm sorry…" Lexi paused, hoping that she'd be able to produce his name with the added pinch of a little pressure, but floundered, came up with nothing, and just plowed on. "I just have a lot on my mind."

"Really?" he asked, slamming down some more of his drink. "Because you don't look like a woman who has a ton to turn over in that pretty little head of yours."

In that moment, Lexi's mind went blank. With rage.

"Was that supposed to be a compliment, Roy?"

"It's Ray," he snapped. "And of course it was a compliment. I called you pretty."

"Sounded more like you called me dumb."

"If that's the way you want to take it," he shrugged facing halfway away from her. He burst out, a little louder than he'd been the rest of the evening. "God! Why are women always so sensitive?"

"Maybe because you call them dumb." Lexi stood.

Suddenly, his hand was banded around the sensitive skin of her upper arm, too tight. "Wait a minute, you're just up and leaving after I tanked my entire night talking to you? I bought you that drink!" He gestured angrily toward her empty glass.

Lexi pinched one of his fingers between hers and twisted aggressively. He quickly unhanded her, but now he was standing too.

"You mean that five-dollar glass of crappy whiskey? Newsflash Ron, women don't owe you shit even if you shell out for them. And even if in some twisted world I *did* owe you? Well, consider my debt paid after the fortieth consecutive minute of you slobbering all over Matt Damon's—"

"Ray? Ray Fogerty? Is that you?" A masculine hand came down and landed squarely on Ray's shoulder. Ray's knees immediately buckled under the force of the greeting and he was effectively seated back on his bar stool. "Man, I haven't seen you since I came back to town."

Lexi's eyes followed the hand still clamped to Ray's shoulder to the muscular forearm, to the very attractive elbow, and up to the broad shoulder of the man with the ice blue eyes. He loomed over her from behind and in fact, she could feel the heat of his chest against her back. She shivered and fought the urge to sink back into his warmth. He was a stranger and, as was apparent from her interaction with Ray, the last chance she'd taken on a stranger hadn't gone so hot.

"Yeah, how's it going, Eric?" Ray grumbled into his beer, effectively subdued by the man standing behind Lexi.

"It's going well. Really well. Couldn't help but notice things had gotten a little tense over here," the man, Eric, was saying.

Lexi craned her head back so that she could look Eric in the face. "Tension is apparently my middle name these days," she said to him and a grin lit up his face.

"You got a first name to go with that?" he asked.

"Lexi."

"Ray, I'm going to go ahead and take Lexi here off your hands, free up your evening for you."

Ray didn't even look back. The tips of his ears turned pink but he swallowed down the rest of his beer and pulled out some bills to pay his tab.

In a moment, Ray was gone and Eric sat in his seat. He handed his empty glass over to the pretty little bartender and it was almost like Ray had never even been there.

"Presto change-o," Lexi said, then made the sound-effect of a foot slipping on a banana peel. She was feeling a little loose tonight. From the whiskey and from all the changes in her life.

"I'm sorry?" Eric asked her as he wordlessly ordered both of them another round.

"Oh, nothing," Lexi replied, waving it away. "You just switched with Ray so fast it was a 'presto change-o'! And that reminded me of this old cartoon called 'Presto Change-o'. Where there's all sorts of sound effects like that." She made the banana peel sound again.

"Sure, I remember that," Eric said, his eyes crinkling at the corners as he smiled down at her. He made a sad trombone sound that made Lexi laugh in delight. "What kind of animal was that character again, from the cartoon?"

"A cat, I think?"

"Could have been a bear."

"No, he had a long tail. Remember the girl did too. She could swing it in a circle, like she was spinning a lasso and drawling 'c'mere big boy'."

This time Eric was the one laughing. "Gotta say, so

far tension really does not seem like your middle name."

Lexi visibly deflated.

"Yikes," Eric grimaced. "Welp, my new life goal is to never make you make that face again."

"Well, I was feeling pretty good until you reminded me," she said as she playfully poked his side. She tried to keep her eyes from falling out of her head when she met rock where there should have been belly. "I've got this big move ahead of me and this morning I had to sell something I loved to make it happen. I'm just... down. And stressed."

"What did you have to sell?" he asked, and then widened his eyes comically. "Was it your body? Or better yet, your virginity? Did you auction it off to the highest bidder?" He laid a hand on her arm. "Am I just hours too late?"

Lexi found herself laughing again as she playfully swatted his hand away. She wasn't usually this silly, and certainly not with a man she'd just met. Must be something in the air. "More like half a decade too late. I 'auctioned' that prize off to Steve Jessup for the high price of two tickets to a Radiohead concert on our three-week anniversary." Eric's grin made Lexi's stomach dip. "What about you?"

"When did I 'auction off my flower'?" Eric asked. He scrunched his face up in memory. "Hmmmm. Well, it was to Shawny Lowenschuss. And she won that one off me with the high, high bid of looking damn fine in her cheerleader uniform."

"Cheerleader, ugh." Lexi face palmed and then ran her fingers around the rim of her glass. "You would."

"I did," he agreed, waggling his eyebrows at her.

And just like that, she was laughing again. Something she hadn't had cause to do in way too long. The stress of the last few months had been starting to be unbearable. Because she sent every other paycheck to her dad, she just couldn't seem to get her feet under her. Her dreams had never seemed further away.

"Thank you, Marina," Eric said to the bartender as she set their drinks down. And then, to the surprise of both women, Eric leaned forward, grabbed Marina by the chin and planted a quick kiss on her very shocked lips. Lexi's laughter died in her throat. What the hell? All that flirting and then he just up and kisses the bartender?

Marina stepped back, gave him a little, confused smile and sort of floated toward the kitchen.

"Uuuuuuuhhhhhh." It was all Lexi managed to get out.

"I'm not into her," Eric said quickly. "I've known her my whole life. But tonight I learned something new about her. And I just wanted to stir it up. Get things going."

"What?" Lexi asked, completely confused.

Eric waggled his fingers down the bar toward a very handsome man with dark hair and dark eyes who currently flipping Eric the bird. The man stood abruptly and disappeared through the kitchen doors where Marina had just gone. Eric lifted his glass in their direction in a silent salute. "Dylan sometimes needs a little kick in the ass to get up and do something."

"Or he needs a little kiss on the lips, rather," Lexi said, raising one eyebrow.

"Jealous?" Eric asked her, a cocky grin on his lips.

But Lexi didn't get a chance to answer before Dylan came storming back out of the kitchen, threw some bills on the counter and rounded the bar toward them.

"Real cute, Eric," Dylan snapped. "You're the one who pulls that crap and somehow she still thinks it's my fault."

Unable to resist, Lexi reached up, grabbed Dylan by the chin, and planted a smacking kiss right on his lips. He blinked at her, nonplussed, as she plopped back down on her bar stool.

Eric's mouth fell right open.

"We're even now," Lexi told Eric as a grin spread over Dylan's face.

"I think we are too," Dylan said to Eric. "Nice to meet you, I'm Dylan Quinn."

"Lexi Fischer." They shook hands. "You having girl problems, Dylan Quinn?"

He shrugged, hands jammed into his pockets. "None that I need my friends to solve."

"Fair enough," Lexi said as she raised her drink to him. But she noticed his eyes darkened considerably when Marina came back out of the kitchen, carrying a tray of burgers and fries.

"I'm going to head home," Dylan said nodding at both of them and turning to jet out of the restaurant.

Lexi bet he had no idea that Marina's eyes followed him the whole way.

Lexi turned back to Eric to tell him her observation when she realized he was still staring at her, mouth open.

"You just kissed my friend," he said.

"Trust me. It wasn't a hardship. He's very good looking," Lexi said, pretending to try and get a last glimpse of him through the crowd.

Eric planted a single finger on the bottom of her chin and tilted her head back around so that she was facing him. She just barely suppressed the shiver it sent down her spine to have him command her so easily. She was partial to a man with a certain amount of gravitas. A little bit of *doing what I say is its own reward*. "You still stressed, Lexi?"

"A little," she answered. The truth was, being around him was relaxing her. But that didn't change the steaming pile of crap her life had become.

Eric leaned in a little closer. Lexi found herself automatically mirroring the motion. The whole "music/other people/world fade away" thing happened again. And Lexi found herself in a lovely little whirling tunnel with the most handsome man she'd ever seen in real life.

"I can think of one really great way to eliminate your stress," he said in a low, gravelly voice.

Lexi laughed, tossing her hair over her shoulder and leaning in further. "Oh, I just bet you could."

"Might get sweaty though," he said, pulling a glossy

chunk of her hair through his fingers. "Might be a little rough for a girl as delicate as you."

Suddenly, the joke was over and Lexi's heart started to pound as her mind spun out wild images of what he was whispering to her. The two of them, tangled and sweaty in the back of her car in the parking lot. Or in the bathroom of the bar. Or, fuck it, right here, right now. Lexi took a swig of her drink. It had obviously been a little bit too long for her. She had to calm down.

"I don't think I've ever been described as delicate before," she said, and even though she was flirting, it was the truth. She was strong, direct. And often described as intimidating.

He leaned back a little, but his knees came around either side of hers, caging her in. "So, you think you could handle some pounding?"

Wow. Was it just her or had the heat suddenly gone up in here? "Excuse me?"

He grinned yet again. "You ever taken down a wall with nothing but a mallet and all the rage you never get to let out of the cage?"

"Excuse me?" she repeated.

"I just bought a ranch, about a mile from here. There's an old barn that I've been demolishing and let me tell you, it sure beats therapy."

Lexi leaned back, a surprised little smile blooming over her face. "You're serious."

"As a rattlesnake bite." He threw some bills on the counter. "You coming?"

She cocked her head to one side, studying him. He sure was handsome. His body was lean and cut and he had the face of a Greek god. Aristocratic. Except for that big old grin that cracked it right in two. And those eyes. Bluer than the sky on a clear day. "Let me hit the ladies real quick."

Eric nodded and smiled, indicating he would wait. She slid off the barstool and wove through the bar toward the bathrooms. Halfway there, she crossed paths with the bartender.

Lexi tapped her on the shoulder. "Hey."

Marina turned around and instantly paled. "I'm not dating him. He's all yours. I have no idea on earth why he kissed me. I—"

"Hey, hey!" Lexi held up her hands when she realized that the woman thought she was about to go psycho on her or something. "Water under the bridge, girly. Takes a lot more than that to get me fighting in a bar. Actually," Lexi cocked her head to one side, pretending to think really hard. "I don't think anything could get me fighting in a bar."

Marina gave her a relieved smile. "Then, is there something I could help you with? You want to order a drink?"

"No," Lexi said. "I guess I just wanted to ask about him." She nodded her head toward where Eric waited for her at the bar. "Leaving with him. Safe? Not safe? Should I make an appointment to get my brain scanned instead? Woman to woman, what do you think?"

Marina looked toward Eric and didn't even take a half a second before she answered. "Safe. Great idea. Even greater guy. You hooked yourself one of the good ones."

And just like that, Marina was melting back behind the bar to keep working and Lexi was smiling harder than she had in a very long time.

2

So, Eric noted as he drove up the twisty mountain road toward his ranch, yet another thing that was different in Montana. Picking up a woman. In L.A. it was all ritz and flash. Impressive, expensive liquor. Sliding her into the buttery leather seats of his Maserati. Zooming off into the glittery Hollywood night together. Ending up in his fancy glass house or in hers.

Not that he'd done that in about six years. Not since before... Nope. He wasn't going to think about Brianne anymore tonight. Not while he had Lexi sitting shotgun in his truck, the windows rolled down and the velvety Montana sky looking so close and so far at the same time.

He watched as Lexi shifted in her seat, her fingers tapping out a rhythm on her leg. Her very pretty leg. Her very distracting leg. Eric whipped his eyes back to the road.

She was nervous, he could tell. And why wouldn't she be? She'd just left civilization with a man she didn't know.

And now he was driving her up a mountain in the dead of night. He wanted to put her at ease.

"Best part's coming up," he told her and tried not to wince when she jumped at his sudden voice.

"What?"

"The best part of the drive to my ranch, it's coming up in T minus five, four, three, two aaaaaand bam." He firework-fluttered his hand as if he were presenting a magic trick as the car slid around a curve, out of a stand of trees, and the mountain fell away. Below them, a dark valley opened up and rolled for miles. The sky was suddenly five times as big as it had looked before.

"Whoa," Lexi muttered. "I think we just stumbled into a galaxy far, far away." She leaned forward over the dashboard to peer out the windshield toward the expansive night sky.

"I know. It's crazy beautiful," Eric agreed. "You ever notice how some night stars are just stars? And some nights they just…" He shrugged. "I can't explain it."

"No," Lexi said, and Eric was pleased when she put one of her Chuck Taylors up on the dashboard. It meant she was more comfortable. "I think I get what you're saying. There are some nights that you look at the stars and they remind you that they're stars. Because, you know, duh. But then there are some nights that you look at them and they remind you that you're standing on a planet. One tiny planet in the whole expansive universe."

"Exactly!" He couldn't believe that she'd understood what he was talking about so well. "And not just a tiny planet. But it also reminds you that you're an even tinier person." He held up his finger and thumb an inch apart.

Lexi reached up and pinched his fingers even closer together, her glittery rings flashing in the dark. "More like that."

Eric grinned as he felt a warmth shoot from her hand to his. "See those lights down there? The two bluish ones and the orange one in between?"

Lexi sat up, looked where he was pointing. "Yeah."

"That's my ranch. Those are the porch lights for the homestead. And that fourth light over there, that's where you're going to show me your awesome demo skills."

"You're really tearing down a whole barn? Why?"

Eric grimaced. "Termite damage."

"Yikes."

"Yeah, but the ranch owner was honest about it, and tearing it down and rebuilding is a small price to pay given the plans I have for the land. The house is alright though. I'm already mostly moved in."

"So you're fixing it up to turn it into…" she prompted.

Eric turned the car down a small dirt road, the last twisting ride down the mountain until they got down onto the flatter land where his ranch was.

"A horse ranch."

Lexi made a little noise that Eric couldn't begin to interpret. He thought it might be half delight and half sadness. He paused, waiting for her to elaborate, but when she didn't, he plowed right on.

"Yeah, I've got about fifty acres, so I could have a fair number of horses."

"Maybe less than you think," Lexi said, staring out into the darkness. "It depends on a lot of factors, what kind of soil you're on, terrain, foliage."

"You know a lot about horses?" He peered at her curiously through the dark as he steered his truck down the long, skinny driveway that split his land in half.

Lexi shrugged, sadness lancing across her face for a second before she hid it beneath a confident smirk. "I know a lot about a lot of things. Are you raising the horses for racing?"

"Could be. Not quite sure of the plan yet. Maybe once I get the hang of ranching, I'll turn it into a B and B. Give city folks a taste of the simple life."

Lexi squinted at him. "Pretty big financial commitment to not be sure of the plan."

Eric pulled the truck up to the barn. He'd been pretty sure that she didn't know who he was back at the bar. Not that he was famous or anything, but some women made a point of recognizing a billionaire's face. If she thought this was a big monetary risk for him, then she didn't know he was Eric Davenport, wasn't with him for his money, and he definitely liked that.

In L.A., he was Eric Davenport, billionaire. Here in Montana, he was Eric Davenport, kid who came for the summers, got rich and fancy in California, and came back to find the good life.

Right now, to Lexi, he was just Eric.

And in a weird way, telling Lexi he was a billionaire didn't feel right, but neither did telling her he was just an aspiring ranch owner.

Still, maybe that was his own identity issue rearing its ugly head. He was moving on, yes, but in some ways, he didn't even recognize who he was anymore.

"Right now I'm running my grandparents' hardware store in town while they're on vacation," he finally said. "So I've got a pretty steady income." A version of the truth, yes, but would he tell her more? Maybe, but at this point he didn't even know if there was a reason to. Right now, Lexi was just an attractive woman he'd met at a bar. One who had piqued his interest more than any other woman had in a long time.

Lexi nodded and jumped down from the truck like a pro. "Lucky duck. I find myself working like a dog to save up but somehow the money just seems to trickle through my fingers. Not that I'm a spend-thrift or anything, but there always seems to be that unexpected bill, you know?"

He walked with her, side by side, to the big, decrepit barn. The moonlight silvered the rotting wood, making it look almost like a pirate ship spearing out of his dark yard. Although he'd never had to struggle for money, he nonetheless understood the concept of being blindsided. Of your life taking an unexpected detour. He wondered what Lexi's detours had been, and had just opened his mouth to ask her when she cocked her hip. Her shiny hair tumbling over one slim shoulder, she held up one finger, and her rings winked at him. "But wait a second. I thought we were out here to help me relieve a little tension, not to discuss my credit score."

The business man inside Eric had him briefly wondering what her credit score was, but the man inside him wondered what her ass in those jeans would look like when she was swinging that mallet in the barn.

Grinning, Eric grabbed her hand and tugged her toward the barn.

"Wow, this thing is straight out of Children of the Corn," Lexi murmured, stumbling after Eric and pulling cobwebs out of her hair.

"I know," he grinned even wider, pulling her over to the back wall of the barn that was already mostly torn away. They could see the dark mountain looming over the valley through the ragged hole. He walked to the corner and picked up the sledge hammer he'd been using earlier. He held it out to Lexi.

"I'm telling you. This is better than yoga."

She raised an eyebrow, but took the hammer out of his hands. "What do you know about yoga?"

Now he was the one raising the eyebrow. "I lived in L.A. for most of my life. Trust me. I can *chaturanga* you under the table."

Lexi tried not to smile. "Maybe we'll have to test that little theory."

"Anytime, anywhere. But first, stop stalling. Let's do this."

"Sounds easy," Lexi shrugged, striding over to the wall and raising the hammer behind her head.

Eric caught her wrist in one large palm before she could swing more than an inch. "No, come on. You jump in like that, you take all the romance out of it."

Lexi let out a surprised laugh and turned to face him. "Romance? In smashing a wall?"

"Sure," Eric shrugged his shoulders. "There's romance in everything. Trust me. You put a little effort into it, seduce the wall a little bit, the pay off is way higher."

Now Lexi was really laughing. "You want me to wine and dine the wall? Yawn and slide my arm over its shoulders at the drive-in?"

He smiled too, took her by the shoulders and spun her to face the wall. The pressure of his hands was light, but constant. He stood just close enough for her to feel the heat of his body. He resisted the urge to slide his fingers over the smooth skin of her shoulders.

"Ok. Stay with me here, Lexi. That wall is not a wall. It is the physical representation of every shitty thing in your life. Every appointment you've been late to. Every nosy neighbor. Every flat tire."

She cocked her head back to look at him and the movement made one of the straps of her tank top slide over his thumb. "Those are not my problems, Eric."

"Well, either you can tell me your problems so I can really help you visualize, or you can just fill in the blanks in your own head."

She nodded, but kept her lips pressed firmly closed and Eric found himself vaguely disappointed that she wasn't telling him what had her so stressed out.

"Alright, I'm visualizing," she said.

"Ok, so picture those problems playing on that wall like a movie from a projector. And when you take the hammer to that wall, those problems will shatter into the night."

"Yeah," she whispered and Eric knew that she'd been taken in by his words.

"Don't just swing the hammer," he told her. "Use every muscle in your body. Start from here." He dropped one of his hands to her stomach, felt the warmth of her tight belly through her thin shirt. "You're going to twist back and feel it burn in here. And then you'll feel it here." He slicked one hand up the sleek line of her spine, almost all the way to her hairline. "Your shoulders will be next." Two hands lightly over her shoulders, down to her elbows. "Even your hands, tight over the handle, they'll feel it too." He clamped his hands over hers for just a second. "You'll plant your feet." He tapped the outside of each of her shoes with his own. "And then you'll swing. All your frustration, all your stress, you'll draw it out of you like water out of a well. And it'll burn. Trust me. It kind of tears its way out of your muscles. But then you'll smash the shit out of that wall. And you'll feel a hell of a lot lighter. Freer."

Her breaths had turned into panting gasps. And so had his own. His heart was racing, as if it were trying to jump the two-inch gap between his chest and her back.

She stepped away from him, closer to the wall, and he

immediately missed the raw heat kicking off her body. He was almost hypnotized by her as she stepped forward, choking up on the mallet like a baseball player. She planted her feet, just like he'd told her, and swung for the fences.

Eric's eyebrows lifted into his hairline. He was majorly impressed. She'd needed no test swings to get her bearings. The hammer exploded through the wall with a resounding bang. The old barn echoed with it as she prepared to swing again.

This time when the mallet connected, boards flung ten feet from the wall as an entire section of the barn shook with the force of her hit. Lexi let out a little satisfied noise that had Eric shifting his pants to get more comfortable.

She looked beautiful, was all he could think. She stood there in the blue shadows of the old barn, her arms bare and contoured with muscle. Her hair rained down her back. She had almost a coltish look, long and graceful, a body free of adornment except for the rings on her fingers. Studying her, Eric got the impression that she was a woman who was used to doing things. Putting her body to use. She had none of the delicate, refined look of the women he knew in L.A. Women whose bodies were more of a canvas for their own beauty art projects. Nothing wrong with that, of course. But there was something very appealing about this woman in her tank top and jeans, no makeup and sneakers. Something very appealing indeed about a woman who held a tool like she'd used one before.

And something painfully appealing about her ass in

those jeans. Good lord. The woman had a perfect ass. Eric ruthlessly ripped his eyes away from it when she turned back to him, panting with delight and smirking when she realized what he'd been looking at.

* * *

Lexi cocked one hip out, playfully giving Eric a better view of her ass. He deserved to be rewarded for an idea as good as this one. The man was letting her destroy his barn for her own catharsis.

And it was working.

She was looser than she'd felt in years. She'd pictured her bank account on that wall. Working three jobs for the last two years and still having to kiss Maple goodbye that morning. She'd pictured her father giving up all his dreams just to give her a good life. A stable life.

That thought had Lexi turning away from Eric again. Back to the wall. She raised the sledge hammer behind her, squinted her eyes at the wall and pictured it there. Her father's face, so handsome, so kind. She pictured him as he looked in pictures as a young man. Movie star good looks and all the hope in the world. He'd wanted to be an actor. Go to Hollywood. But her mother had gotten pregnant with her and he'd stuck around. Chosen his daughter and raised her right. Lexi swung the hammer. And she wasn't smashing through her father's image. She was smashing through the image of all the dreams, the ambition that he'd given up.

She'd spent years figuring out how to be thankful for it while never wanting it to happen to her.

Lexi raised the hammer again, a thin sweat starting to break out over her skin. She could hear Eric shifting behind her, his boots on the gravel. A quiet sound, but one that reminded her he was there. Not that she needed much reminding. Her body was still buzzing from each place he'd touched her. His hand on her stomach. Up her spine and over her arms. Even his shoes on either side of hers. Each touch, seemingly so innocent, had lit her up. Woken her up. Every touch had zinged along her blood so that it had all melted together into one buzzy cloud of energy.

Sexual energy zipped through her, giving her a strength she barely knew she had. Smashing the wall in front of her wasn't going to dissipate it, she suddenly realized.

Only one thing would—touching the man behind her.

He was the kind of man you were lucky to have one night with in your life. Somebody you reminisced about screwing when you were old and rocking on a front porch. She wouldn't usually have done anything like this, but here she was, smashing through her stress and considering jumping the bones of a man she'd just met.

But first things first. Lexi wasn't going to waste this opportunity. She called up the last images she needed to smash through. A kaleidoscope of all the things that could keep her from her dreams. Every sticky spider web that life had to offer. Confusing, because some were as good as they were bad. Going broke was right up there with falling in love. Entanglements that could keep her here in Nowhere, USA. Illness, a broken down car, a very handsome man…

A man like Eric.

A man she couldn't get involved with.

At least, for more than a night.

But for tonight, could she do it?

Could Eric be her goodbye present to herself?

It wasn't like her to turn to him and toss down the sledge hammer. It wasn't like her, breathing hard, to stare him in the eye as she paced toward him. It wasn't like her to peel the tank top right off her body.

And it certainly wasn't like her to grab him by the back of his neck, hitch her legs up around his waist and drink from his mouth like it was the finest whiskey.

But she did all those things. Before the buzz could wear off. Before her head could catch up to her.

Eric's hands immediately found her ass. His touch was strong and sure, nothing tentative. Lexi couldn't get enough of it. His hands on her felt like anchors holding her in place. Without his touch, she felt like she might just spin right off the earth.

"The house," Eric murmured ripping his mouth from hers.

"Too far," she said back, raking her sensitive lips over the stubble on his chin. "Right here."

He growled low in his throat and took her lips again, his strong tongue seeking out hers. Their flavors mixed. One strong, one delicate, and neither could get enough.

When his mouth dropped to her neck, to her collarbone, Lexi arched and let her head drop back. Seconds later he was setting her feet down on the ground and spinning her around.

Lexi shivered as he ran his hands down her arms the same way that he had when he'd been talking to her about smashing the wall. His front pressed into her back as he tangled his fingers with hers, lifted her hands and planted her palms on an old wooden beam in front of her.

He didn't use anything to restrain her, but Lexi felt pinned in place. She could feel his hands on her body even when he wasn't touching her. His hands worked back up her arms and over her back, tracing her spine. And then they graced over her belly. In a solid, sure movement, Eric's hands went from her hipbones, up to cup the bottom of her breasts and back down.

She shivered as his fingers skimmed the waistband of her jeans and his mouth landed on the back of her neck.

With a swift move he swept her hair off her back and groaned.

"Jesus," he murmured, more to himself than to her. "So beautiful."

He unclipped her bra and slid it down her arms, planting her hands back on the beam when he was done. And then her breasts were falling into his hands as he nipped at the lobe of one of her ears.

Lexi was unprepared for the electricity she felt when his thumbs raked over her nipples. She'd been with guys before, sure. But she'd never felt anything like this.

And then the heat of him was gone and she whimpered. Lexi's eyes fluttered open, the air suddenly cool around her. Immediately, he ducked under her arms and fell to his knees in front of her. Reverently, he flipped the button on her jeans then pulled them down her hips.

There were a million things she could have said in that moment, but all she could do was feel and feel and feel. The scrape of her jeans over her hips, his strong, sure hands at her ankles, helping her step out of her shoes and jeans, and then the stubble on his chin as he dragged it up the inside of her leg.

Lexi gasped as he nipped at the inside of her thigh. He grinned up at her in the silvery shadows of the barn and nipped at the other side.

She was certain that her heart was going to beat out of her chest. Her breaths came in ragged puffs. Wearing only her underwear now, her hands clenched at the beam in front of her.

"Lexi." His voice was deep and gruff and literally made her toes curl. "I want to kiss you here." One of his hands touched feather light over her core. She whimpered and spread her legs further apart. A grin flashed across his face but he kept going. "And then I'm going to suck on you here and here." Again, his thumbs electrified her nipples and she couldn't help but arch into him. He hooked his thumbs into the sides of her panties and started inching them down her legs.

"And then what?" she asked breathlessly.

His gaze collided with hers as he helped her out of her

underwear, one strong hand on her ankles at a time. He ran his calloused palm up one of her legs before grabbing her at the knee and tossing her leg over his shoulder.

He was so handsome and so dangerous as he stared up at her, half of his face in the moonlight and half in shadow. His hair tousled, his shoulders stretching his shirt to the limit.

"If you can still speak after, *you're* going to tell me what's next." He licked his lips and reached up for one of her hands, still gripping the beam. "You're going to want to hold on there and here." He dropped her hand into his own hair, tipped her hips forward and dove in.

* * *

She tasted like a piece of fruit, Eric thought. Hot and ripe and bursting on his tongue. He'd always liked going down on a woman, but this was hand's down the most erotic experience of his life. Lexi gripped his hair, shivering against him, her leg like a vice over his shoulder. He'd never seen a woman lose herself like she was doing, her hair cascading almost to the floor as her head bent back.

"Oh," she moaned, like she couldn't believe what was happening. "Oh, god."

Eric had always wanted to please the women he was with, of course he had, but with Lexi, he *needed* her pleasure. He tasted her and tasted her, circling her perfect little clit with his tongue, suckling when the need for her overcame him.

She was panting, moaning, grinding herself against him and it made Eric groan. The feel of her. The coltish, whipping energy of her. One of those mile-long legs over his shoulder, she was a goddess as he let his eyes trail up her body. Her breasts were perfect and full, bouncing with each thrust of her hips as she rode his face. He wanted her orgasm more than he wanted to wake up tomorrow morning. He would swallow it down if it killed him.

He suckled and suckled at her, groaning at her flavor, the slick, soft feel of her. And then his tongue was inside her, lapping at every slide of heaven he found there. Lexi cried out and she stiffened as her channel clenched and clenched at his tongue. He never stopped, drove her right through her orgasm and to the other side.

"Eric," she said, halfway between a moan and a pant. "Eric."

Rising up further onto his knees, he steadied her. Put her foot back on the ground and her hand back on the beam. He was big enough that with her leaned down just a little, he was eye level with her breasts.

He barely gave her a moment to recover before his mouth was on her there. Greedily suckling on her electrified body. He was relentless, using every tool at his disposal. Teeth, stubble, his hands. He knew she would be sensitive after her orgasm and he used that. He wanted her writhing, begging. He wanted her to feel him everywhere in the morning.

He suckled at her until she cried out, halfway between pushing forward and pulling away.

"I need…Oh god…"

"Tell me, sweetheart," he growled, his fierce eyes piercing into her blurry ones. "Tell me what you need."

She trembled where she stood and Eric instantly rose, stepping behind her to steady her. He ran a hand over her back like she was a filly he needed to calm. And it worked.

She took a deep breath and tipped her head to one side, her hands still gripping the beam like the good girl he knew she was. "I need you."

He slicked his hand over her again. "Tell me, sweetheart. Where do you need me?"

Her lips trembled, but her eyes found his. "Inside me," she whispered.

Well, she didn't have to tell him twice.

Eric instantly whipped the shirt off over his head, kicked his shoes off, and stepped out of his pants and briefs. He grabbed a condom out of his pants pocket and slicked it on.

He felt a surge of pride when Lexi took him in, head to toe.

"Wow," she whispered to herself, her eyes landing on his cock. Which was looking pretty fucking happy to be the hell out of his pants and less than an inch away from this gorgeous woman's dripping wet slice of heaven.

His size could be intimidating to a lot of women and he didn't want her to worry. He grasped her hands, pressed her palms even more firmly into the beam so she'd have something to balance herself on, then planted his hands on her hips, pulling her toward him.

The movement bent her over and Lexi automatically let her head drop forward. He didn't like that he couldn't see her eyes. But he didn't have any other complaints about the view. Her back was as smooth as ice, silvery and long. Her ass was round and spread and singing a siren song to his cock.

Eric stepped forward, pressing himself against her core. Touching as much of her skin as he could in this position. He lined up their legs and planted his hands on her hips.

And saw stars when the head of his cock speared through her silkiness. He didn't push inside her yet, just pushed his cock forward, her pussy lips wetting the condom.

Lexi gasped and pushed against him so he did it again. And again. Her pussy fucking the side of his cock over and over. When her breaths started panting and her legs tightening, Eric decided that he couldn't take anymore. He would lose his mind if he didn't get inside her.

Pulling back slowly, so she'd know his intentions, Eric used one of his hands to position his cock at her entrance. He pushed in just an inch and Lexi moaned, loud and long.

"More," she gasped when he didn't push in any further.

But he couldn't, not yet. He was too busy tightening the leash around his neck. It wouldn't do to shove her down and fuck her like an animal, and that was the only thing his body was telling him to do right now.

"More, Eric. God, please," she moaned and he couldn't resist when she begged so pretty like that. He pushed forward and she swallowed him whole.

His vision tunneled at the feel of her. So wet and tight. He felt like she was branding him. There was no going back from a pussy like that. Nothing would ever be the same.

He pulled out a little and thrust back in experimentally. He didn't want to blow too soon and he wasn't sure how much of this he could handle. The feel of her, the sight of her, her scent. But then she moaned, so perfectly, so pretty, and he found that he couldn't deny her anything. He started a rhythm, perfect, hard. Each stroke was long and fluid; he wanted her to feel every inch of him.

Lexi threw her head back and he caught a glimpse of her face. Her mouth open and her eyes glazed and blurry. She screamed his name again before grinding her hips back onto his, taking his strokes from fluid to sharp.

But the movement was too much. Her hands slipped from the beam and they tumbled down. Eric softened their fall and she ended up on her hands and knees, Eric over her, still ten inches deep.

He didn't have any complaints about that and neither did she. He fucked her from behind, their rhythm barely missing a beat. He planted his hands on either side of hers so that her back was completely covered by his chest as he rutted into her. His mouth fell to her ear and instead of kissing her, he found himself whispering.

"God, you feel so good, sweetheart." The words tumbled out of his mouth. "You're so pretty when you come. So perfect. You going to come for me again, sweetheart? You going to come on this cock?"

Lexi moaned at his words, her pussy tightening involuntarily. And when she threw her head back, she bared her neck to Eric and he gladly dropped his mouth there. He could feel her scream in her throat, under his lips, as she bore down and came and came. It went on forever this time, her body tight and vibrating. He licked a long line up her neck and back down. And then there was nothing to do but clamp his teeth over her shoulder, hold her in place to take everything he was giving her as he rutted her through her orgasm.

When it ended, he sensed that his weight was too much for her.

And he was done with that anyways.

"Your face," he murmured. "I need to see your face."

He pulled out of her and instantly went to his back. Not caring about the dirt floor of the barn. All he could think about was her. For those moments, she was his entire world.

* * *

Lexi was on another planet. She'd never come through intercourse before and it was the best orgasm she'd ever had. She thought she could have come from his words alone, but then there was his monster cock inside her, doing the dirtiest things imaginable. Oh god, this man was trouble. But she couldn't, wouldn't stop herself. She whimpered when she felt him pull out. But then she felt his hands tugging on her hips and dragging her on top of him.

He wanted her to ride him. Yes. Yup. Let's go.

She'd never been more eager for anything in her life. Lexi straddled him, positioning herself over his cock and taking him in. He was big—it would never be an easy fit—but she was so wet from coming like a nuclear bomb that he slid right to the hilt.

His eyes practically rolled back in his head.

"Yes," he ground out through clenched teeth, his hands digging into her hips. And now it was her turn to take him apart piece by piece.

Lexi lifted up off him and then back down. Setting a pace that had her biting her lip against the pleasure. Good god, was it possible she was going to come again? What was it with him and his magical cock? Her strokes were fast and soft and he groaned through his clenched teeth, his head falling back.

"Oh Christ," he growled. "You're going to kill me."

And then his hands stilled her hips, holding her in place as he slammed up to meet her, thrusting into her from below.

Lexi's head fell back as her body tightened. It was happening again. It was happening. It was—

Lights exploded in front of her eyes and she felt pulses of pleasure through her fingertips and even the ends of her hair. She was nothing but white, vibrating light as she came and came and came. Her orgasm doubled, tripled. She felt him everywhere. On her skin as well as inside her. She pictured him kneeling in front of her, swallowing her down. And how he'd looked, his feet between hers, as he'd fucked her standing up. She heard once again his dirty words in her ear when he'd taken her on her hands and knees.

She forced her eyes open and burned the image into her brain. Eric on his back, fucking her from below, his face tight and straining, his strokes erratic and harsh. And then his eyes found hers, his pupils dilated and he grew even harder inside her.

Lexi whimpered as his cock swelled even larger and his orgasm overtook him. She was still coming, and she rode that feeling, his orgasm and hers smashing together, until she couldn't anymore. Finally, she collapsed on top of him.

It might have been ten minutes or an hour before their heart rates evened out. Before they had enough breath to speak. For a moment, Lexi struggled against the urge to say how awed she was. Moved.

Better to keep things light.

"You've got some face, Eric," she said, leaning over him, her hair tickling his chest. "Like Paul Newman in Butch Cassidy and the Sundance Kid."

"Come on." He shifted underneath her, his hands falling away from her ass for the first time in an hour. He raked one hand through his hair, before dropping the hand to her back in a light caress.

He was embarrassed by her words and she couldn't be more delighted. "No, I'm serious. You're beautiful just like he was. You've got that whole carved-from-stone-I-can-see-right-through-you-panty-melter thing that he had going on."

"First of all, Paul Newman was blonde in that movie."

"It was in black and white," she interrupted. "So it's hard to tell."

He ignored her interruption and just plowed right on. "Second of all, I'm not 'beautiful,' I'm rugged. Handsome. The manliest of men."

She bit her bottom lip to keep from smiling. "Sure."

"And third," he continued, once again ignoring her. "You're right about the panty-melter thing."

She laughed as he rolled them over, tangled his hands in her hair and kissed along her neck for a minute.

"And   fourth…"

"There's more? Jeez, Eric, you're a real talker."

"*Fourth*, you've got some face yourself, Lexi Fischer." He caressed his knuckles over said face. Firm pressure, nothing delicate. She liked that about him. "Like Sophia Loren in Houseboat. But your hair is long."

Now it was her turn to squirm. "Oh, give me a break. You already melted my panties, Paul Newman, no need to turn on the burners."

"See! It's not so easy when you're the one in the hot seat." He slicked a hand over her side and paused to lean over and look at something. "We're filthy," he grinned, holding up his hand to show how much dirt and muck they'd subjected themselves to. "We need a shower."

And then he was tugging her up off the ground and picking her up like a baby. "My hero," she batted her eyelashes at him. "But you know I can walk, right?"

"Indulge me," he responded. "This is my King Kong moment. You know, 'Me Tarzan.'"

"I believe such an introduction would have been more appropriate *before* you ravished me, Tarzan."

He shrugged, bounding up the front porch of his house. "Can't win 'em all." Then he grinned. "Which is just fine with me considering I'm pretty fucking happy with what I did win."

As he leaned down and kissed her nose, she laughed. "Me, too, Eric. Me, too."

3

A few short hours later, the sun was just starting to wake up and it turned the light in Eric's bedroom gray. They'd fallen asleep only an hour or two ago but already, Lexi was sitting on the edge of his bed, stretching that smooth, beautiful back and tossing her hair up into a messy bun.

"You going somewhere?" Eric asked, only cracking one eye open but unable to resist tracing a hand down her spine.

She jumped a little, turned and looked at him. "I didn't mean to wake you."

Well aware that she hadn't answered his question, Eric forced both eyes open and sat up, the sheets pooling at his waist. He watched as she rose then looked around.

"Damn," she muttered, standing up. "I just realized we left our clothes out in the barn."

He kept his eyes trained on her face, trying to figure out her mood. Usually, he was really good at reading people. In fact, it was one of the many reasons he was so successful in the business world. But as she shifted from one foot to the other, crossed her arms over her chest, he was having a hell of a time pinning her down.

"Dresser," he said to her, motioning to the set of drawers behind her.

She turned and squinted at him through the dark. "You're offering to let me wear some of your clothes?"

"Sure, you can borrow whatever you want." He stretched too, swinging his feet over the edge of the bed.

"Yeah. No, I don't think so. I'll just go get mine."

Now Eric was the one squinting at her. She looked like a deer in the headlights. Nervous, unsteady. He doubted that even she was keeping up with the racing thoughts in her head.

"Alright," he said, raising a hand to show he wasn't going to force her into anything. "You stay here, I'll go get your stuff."

She looked like she was going to argue but she clapped her mouth closed when he stood and sauntered over to pull a pair of shorts out of his drawers. He could feel her eyes follow him and it went a long way toward boosting his confidence. At least she wasn't having second thoughts about whether or not she was attracted to him.

Though she was definitely having second thoughts about something, he reflected as he bounded out of the house and back toward the barn. He grinned as he stepped through the hole in the destroyed wall. He looked over the mallet that lay haphazardly where she'd tossed it. There were muddy marks in the dirt where they'd rolled and grappled and taken from each other. He raised his eyebrows at the distance of each piece of clothing. They'd really gotten their clothes the hell away from their bodies as fast and as hard as they could.

He couldn't remember ever feeling more urgency or passion for somebody in his entire life. Not even Brianne.

They'd been together for six years. She'd been a huge chunk of his life for more than half a decade. For six years he'd loved her, made love to her, planned his life around her. And for six years she'd loved him back. Just not as much as she'd loved Eric's best friend, Gabe.

And for some reason, for the first time, he was beginning to understand how his feelings for Brianne, as much as he'd loved her, hadn't been all they could be.

"Not now," he muttered to himself as he grabbed their clothes off the ground and headed back to the house. He didn't want to think about all that right now. About the reasons he'd left L.A. to move to Montana. He didn't want to focus on the past. Or even think about the past. He wanted his future.

As great as she was, Brianne would never have smashed through a barn wall that way. She'd never have jumped him outside. She'd never have fucked him on the ground.

Not because she'd been a prude but because they hadn't been right for each other.

Not the way Lexi was right for him.

Eric banged through his front door and headed up the

stairs. He paused outside the bedroom for a second, and this time deliberately called up an image of Brianne in his head, once again relieved that doing so didn't break his heart anymore.

Instead, her visage quickly vanished, replaced with images from the night before. Lexi bending over for him. Lexi on her hands and knees. Lexi riding him like a goddess with those soft little strokes that had made his eyes cross.

He grimaced down at the tent he was currently making in his shorts. He needed to calm down, or he was going scare the poor woman off. She was nervous enough this morning without him leading with his monster boner.

He took a deep breath, thought of that one time he'd walked in on his grandma changing clothes, and willed himself back under control. He walked back into his bedroom, then tried not to wince at the way she sat on the bed, feet pulled up to her chest, like she was hiding herself from him.

"They're a little dirty, but wearable," he said holding up her clothes.

She shot him a tight smile, reaching out for them.

Handing them over, he sat next to her on the bed while she wiggled into her outfit.

"You a coffee drinker?" he asked.

She nodded. "I'd suck on some coffee beans right about now."

"Great," he rose.

"On second thought, I'll just grab some once I get

back." Her words were hurried and nervous. He hated it. "Lexi, I don't know you well enough to be able to tell exactly what's going on, but did I do something to make you feel bad or mad or something?"

She immediately bit her lip, a look of chagrin crossing her face. "No," she shook her head. "Kinda the opposite, actually."

He cocked his head to one side. "Care to explain?"

She looked back at him, her eyes trailing down to his bare chest. Suddenly, she was standing, striding over to his dresser and rifling through the drawers. She tossed him a shirt.

"Put that on," she said. "I can't think when you look like that." She waved her hand at his chest like his attractiveness was annoying to her.

He bit his cheek to keep from smiling. Happy that she was talking, and beyond happy that his bare chest was scrambling her brains a little bit.

"You're really great. I like you a lot and last night was…" she cleared her throat. "A hall- of-famer as far as I'm concerned."

Eric couldn't help but grin and nod. "Me too."

She matched his smile for a second. Electricity zipped between them again before her eyes skittered away and her smile faded.

"But I'm leaving town today," she said on a deep exhale, tracing her hands through her hair before she jammed them in her pockets.

Eric's eyebrows rose even as his stomach plummeted.

"For vacation?"

"No," she shook her head. "For good."

His chest constricted, cutting off his breath. "Where to?"

A light pink stained her cheeks. "L.A."

Eric felt his mouth drop open. Of course. Of course he'd feel this amazing connection to her only to learn she was moving to the one place he'd never live again.

"I know, I know." She said, misinterpreting the look on his face. "I don't look like an L.A. kind of girl. And I know it's hard to hack it there. But if I don't do it now…"

Right.

That, at least, was a feeling Eric could relate to. He knew what it was like to jump into something because not doing it meant never doing it. He had a ramshackle barn and 50 acres of land to prove it.

"What's waiting in L.A. for you?"

"I'm a screenwriter," she replied, her cheeks going even pinker. "Well, at least, I *want* to be one. I've written a bunch of stuff on my own. But even with the internet, it's really hard to get it into the hands of the right people. Based on everything I've read, I really need to live in L.A. if I want any chance of making it so…"

She raised her hands and let them drop.

"Makes sense. Where will you be living?"

She jammed her hands even harder into her pockets. "Not sure yet?" She said it like a question.

"Wait, so you're moving to L.A. without a place to live?" He heard the judgment in his voice and immediately wished he could take the words back.

She crossed her arms over her chest. "Well, I'm not going there right away. I'm taking the summer to make my way down there. I need to pick up some odd jobs along the way to raise the money. And hopefully by the time I'm down there, I'll have something lined up."

She shrugged like it was no big deal, but he could see the nerves in her eyes. He also felt a little ray of hope light in his chest. Her timeline wasn't as short as she'd made it seem.

"If you don't need to be in L.A. until the end of the summer, then why are you leaving here today?"

At that, she came back to sit on the bed, tracing her hand through her hair again. "Because I didn't sign up to stay here for the summer. Because I've lived in town after town just like this. And I can tell you one thing they all have in common." She turned to him and her eyes were like bright lights pinning him in place. "Quicksand."

His stomach dropped again. "You mean you're scared you'll get stuck here."

She nodded and looked away, playing with the frayed hem of her jeans. "There's a million ways that girls like me get stuck in a place like this. Fear. Being broke." She glanced at him again. "A really great guy."

It all clicked into place for him. She hadn't been acting distant and nervous because she didn't like him or want to be around him. But because she *did* like him and *did* want to be around him.

"Ah," he nodded his head in understanding. "What do

you mean 'girls like you'?"

"You know. Broke. Not much family. A handful of friends scattered across the states. Reasonable amounts of talent. A lot of dreams. And a big old bleeding heart that puts everybody before myself."

He wasn't sure she was painting an altogether accurate picture of herself, but he didn't know her well enough to argue.

"So you figure slowly moving south toward L.A. gives you a much higher chance of making it there. Even if you don't make as much money as you would if you held a steady job here. Say, at a hardware store?" He couldn't say why he was offering this to her. He barely knew her. All he knew was that the thought of her leaving so soon was making his chest squeeze. He knew, without a doubt, that if she left that day, he would never see her again. He couldn't stand the thought. Offering her a job was, perhaps, a little pushy. It was a shot in the dark, and if she walked away from it, well, that was her choice.

"Like the one you currently run?" she narrowed her eyes even further.

He shrugged. "Look, I need help over the summer. There's no way I can run it the way my grandparents need me to *and* focus on getting this ranch up and running at the same time. I could hire some teenager who's going to text at the cash register all day. Or I could hire somebody I trust to help me run it with integrity."

She said nothing. Just furrowed her brow and kept playing with the hem of her pants.

He decided to go for broke. "If you're asking my opinion, which I know you weren't, but hey, here it is. Saving up at a steady job, not having to worry about income, or where you're going to live, or whether or not your car is going to start in the morning, all of that makes it far more probable you'll make it to L.A. at the end of the summer. And if you want, I'll fire you in August so you *have* to go."

She grinned at him for just a second before she bit her lip again, nerves and uncertainty taking over.

He turned to her and took her hand in his. "Plus, I lived in L.A. for a long time. So maybe I can help you figure some stuff out."

For the first time that morning, hope lit in her eyes.

"I swear, Lexi," he said, squeezing her hand for emphasis. "I wouldn't contribute to your quicksand. In fact, I'll be your quicksand lifeguard."

She grinned at that one. "Will you wear a whistle and one of those red floaty things?"

He nodded solemnly. "I'll even wear the teeny tiny bathing suit."

She laughed outright now. "I'd like to see that." But then she was biting her lip again. "I need coffee if I'm going to make this decision."

He was tugging her downstairs before she barely even got the words out of her mouth.

He lifted her up onto his kitchen counter and immediately started making the coffee while she looked around.

"Pretty empty in here," she noted.

He shrugged. "I'm still figuring things out." In more ways than one.

She nodded. "I've never been good at decorating either. I pretty much need a toothbrush and a pillow and I'm set."

"Where are you living now?"

Her eyes skittered away from his as she told him the intersection.

He narrowed his eyes and poured her the first cup of coffee he could squeak out of the rapidly filling receptacle. He knew that intersection. "There's only motels over there."

She shrugged. "I only thought I would be in town for a few nights."

"You had an odd job here?"

"No," she cast her eyes down as she took the cup of coffee from him. "It was my horse. Maple. I sold her yesterday to a guy on the other side of town."

Eric couldn't help the noise of distress that eeked its way out of him. She'd sold her horse to be able to afford to make her way to L.A. That's how badly she wanted to go. His heart immediately went out to this woman. "Lexi, say yes to the job. It'll pay well and I swear, it'll only bring your dreams closer. Plus, I could really use the help. It'll be a win win."

She took a huge slug of the coffee, set the cup aside and stared him in the eye. "If I'm working for you, I'm not going to be sleeping with you."

He choked on his own coffee. "I'm sorry?"

"Look. I've been down on my luck enough times in my life that I can't afford to blur the line between being paid for work and being paid for sex. It's not good for my self worth."

"Lexi, I wouldn't be paying you for sex. I swear. You'd be working an honest-to-god job at the store."

"I won't sleep with you while you're my boss," she repeated staunchly.

Eric sighed. "Fair enough. Wouldn't be my first choice, since last night was the hottest thing I've ever experienced, but I'd respect your wishes. The offer is still on the table, sex notwithstanding."

She stared at him like he was a mystery she was trying to solve. "You really are a good guy, aren't you?"

"I sleep just fine at night."

She hopped down from the counter. "So, I'd work for you. You'd help me figure out the best way to start out in L.A. We wouldn't sleep together," she summed up.

"And you'll live here with me," he finished, pretty certain how she was going to react to that one.

"Excuse me?" she stopped in her tracks, raised an eyebrow. "I most certainly will not be living with my boss who I will *not* be sleeping with."

He grinned and raised his hands up. "Alright, alright. Can't blame a guy for trying. But look, just because we won't be sleeping together doesn't mean I want you staying in those sketchy motels by the highway."

She shrugged. "So I'll find a place."

He snapped his fingers and reached for his cell in his pocket. "You know what? I know someone who might want to take you in."

"Who?"

"Marina, the bartender from last night."

Lexi leaned forward on the counter, sipping from her coffee cup. "You plan on kissing her in front of me again?"

Eric fired off the text he'd just composed and grinned up at her. "That wouldn't be very professional of me, now would it?" He leaned over the counter toward her. "Speaking of professional. You don't technically work for me yet, you know."

She bit the inside of her cheek like she was trying to keep from smiling. "We have a gentleman's agreement."

"So I don't even get some celebratory nookie?" he asked hopefully.

She shook her head, swallowing the rest of her coffee.

"Fair enough," he said again, putting their coffee cups in the sink and heading out to his car to drive her to pick up her stuff. He was bummed that they wouldn't be sleeping together again. In fact, he really hoped she changed her mind about that one. But he knew what it was like to chase a dream while the seedier aspects of life chased you. He knew what it was like to live in fear of failure. And he liked this girl enough that he was going do everything in his power to make sure she shook that fear once and for all.

4

What the hell had happened? Lexi flopped back on her bed feeling like Julia Roberts in Pretty Woman. Well. Sort of. She was, after all, staunchly *refusing* to be a whore. So it wasn't the same thing at all really.

But the sudden switch to glitz and glamour was certainly similar to the movie. Not that Marina's house was particularly glitzy. But it was a big step up from the seedy motels she'd been staying in. And about a monster step up from sleeping in the backseat of her car.

Marina had been overjoyed at the idea of a roommate. Well, at least at the idea of somebody to help out with the rent. Lexi hadn't actually seen her yet but they'd talked on the phone and Marina had left her spare keys under a fake rock in the garden.

Lexi propped herself up on her bed. The room was a little plain, but clean. And it had only taken her about 45 seconds to move all her crap from her car inside. She surveyed her little suitcase that she'd tossed halfway into the closet after unpacking her two drawers-worth of clothes. Her old crappy laptop sat on the desk and a cup of water sat on the nightstand beside her.

And that was it.

In the context of the cute little room, with its light yellow walls and a plush creamy bedspread, her meager belongings looked pitiful. Reaching into her back pocket, Lexi pulled out her wallet. From there she peeled out the picture she kept inside.

Lexi was about eight years old, lanky and skinny, her hair in a messy ponytail. She had her legs kicked out in a can-can pose while her dad laughed down at her, one arm around her shoulders. A ratty baseball cap covered most of his handsome face.

Lexi sighed and carefully leaned the picture up against the wall behind the nightstand. Her handsome father. Always hiding that face of his. He'd put aside his dream to act when Lexi was born, and after her mother died, he'd put the dream away permanently. He'd had to rely on skills he'd learned as a kid to be able to put food on the table. That's when he and Lexi had joined the rodeo circuit.

It had been a strange place to grow up, for sure. Lots of sun-hardened men with drinking problems, cheating on their wives back home and smoking two packs a day. But Lexi couldn't help but feel an affection for the circuit. She'd gotten to spend time with her father every day. Gotten to see little stretches of America while traveling with the rodeo. She'd fallen in love with movies in the back of her father's R.V. He'd plug her into a movie whenever things got too rowdy for a little girl. Maybe not the most classically wholesome life, but it had treated her well. She'd learned how to ride a horse. Hell, Maple had been sold to her cheap on her sixteenth birthday from her father's best friend.

But after she'd turned eighteen, she'd longed for more. She'd left, set out to find her own path. Little did she know that she'd spend the next seven years doing a circuit of her own. Bouncing from town to town, job to job. Scraping by while she carved out time to write and ride Maple.

A tear slid down Lexi's cheek. The check the man had written for her horse still burned a hole in her pocket. Lexi hadn't cashed it even though she desperately needed it. The minute that money ended up in her account, it would become real. All of it. Her horse would be gone and she'd be on her way to L.A.

Suddenly she didn't feel ready. Suddenly everything was moving so fast. Without giving it a second thought, she reached for her cell phone. Checking the time, she knew her dad would be getting ready for the big show. If he wasn't riding tonight, he'd be helping some other cowboy get ready. It wasn't the right time for a call. A quick text wouldn't hurt though.

-*Hey Papa*

As always, his reply was immediate.

-*Hey pumpkin, what's shaking?*

-*Not much, just a little sad about Maple.*

And a little confused about the hottest man I've ever met fucking me into next Tuesday. But, of course, she didn't text that part.

-It was a tough decision, kiddo, and you made sure that horse had a good thing going for her. Nothing wrong with that. I love you, kid. But I gotta get on with the show here. I'm next. Wish your old dad good luck and I'll call you tomorrow.

-Love you too, Papa.

Lexi smiled as she thought of her dad in his chaps and cowboy boots, swinging a leg over a horse. He'd given up bull riding a long time ago, after he'd been tossed and broken some ribs and his wrist. After that, he'd decided he couldn't risk his daughter seeing him get trampled like a rag doll. He stuck to calf roping now. Some barrel racing on occasion.

Lexi's smile faded when she pictured the last time she'd seen her father. Smiling as always, but aging far too fast. He was getting older, and he should have already retired from the rodeo life. But he couldn't. Didn't have any other skills to make a living. And Lexi certainly didn't have the money to help. Not yet. Soon, however. Soon she'd write that screenplay, fulfilling her dreams and helping her father at the same time. Giving him an easier life, for once.

Or so she hoped.

God, she loved her father. He had given up everything for her, and she didn't take that for granted. He was her favorite person in the world. Being with him made her smile. As did being with another man…

The image of her father faded away and an image of Eric took his place.

Lord, she couldn't deny that Eric had pretty much fucked a feeling right into her. Some light, slick bubble that was lodged in her chest and wouldn't pop no matter what she did. And that was just something she was going to have to ignore. Because she wasn't looking to settle down. Not now. And not ever with a ranch owner in Montana.

When she finally did settle down, *after* fulfilling her screenwriting dreams, she'd settle with a world-wise L.A. man, maybe a writer himself. He'd know the right people and take her to hole-in-the-wall restaurants where they served authentic food she'd never even heard of. Maybe her dream guy would surf and play the acoustic guitar in the mornings with his feet up on their kitchen table while she drank a cup of coffee and got started on writing. And her father would live close so she could visit him and treat him to little luxuries now and again.

Good movies. Good food.

Good times.

Yeah. That was the life she wanted. She'd grown up with wrangler men. Worn jeans, a week's worth of stubble, a can of Skoal in the back pocket. She knew those men. Men who partied hard, dreamed about things they'd never shoot for and who could calm a nervous filly with just a hand across her mane. Those men were appealing, sure. Nothing sexier than a man in a tight T-shirt and worn jeans. But, Lexi reminded herself, they weren't just made of quicksand, they were stuck in the quicksand themselves.

Something about Eric had seemed different, though, which was why she'd accepted a job from him. Still he wasn't different enough for her to accept a relationship from him. No sir.

"Lexi?" a woman's voice called out as the front door slammed shut.

"In here!" Lexi shouted back, swinging her feet off the edge of the bed and sitting up.

Marina appeared in the doorway and Lexi cocked her head to one side as she studied the other woman. In the bar, with her bartender apron on and things balancing in her hands, Marina had looked like somebody's little sister, filling in for the night. But here, in the light of day, with her thin sweater and perfectly tailored slacks, holding her own fingers delicately in front of her, Marina looked positively transparent. Like a puff of twisting cumulous cloud that might just get blown away in the wind.

Every feature on her was lighter than the next. Her toffee-colored hair just dusted her shoulders, and eyes that Lexi supposed were hazel seemed practically clear in her light fringe of eyelashes. Her nose was small and shapely and her lips, unpainted, were almost the same color as her skin. She was pretty, Lexi realized, but doing her absolute best to be invisible.

"Do you like your room?" Marina asked in a quiet, musical voice.

Lexi nodded her head, bouncing up and down on the

mattress for a quick second. "Comfortable, clean, what's not to like?"

"Good." Marina glanced down at her fingers and then back up at Lexi. "I'm so sorry about something."

Crap. She was getting kicked out already. "What's that?"

Looking like she'd just robbed a bank, Marina twisted her fingers. "I totally forgot to tell you about something and it's totally fine if it means you don't want to live here anymore. I've been getting by alright on the rent. And of course I'll give you your deposit right back and—"

"Spit it out, Marina." Lexi knew her tone of voice was bordering on rude, but this woman was apologizing herself into an early grave and Lexi needed this band aid to be ripped off, like, yesterday.

Marina worried her lip between her teeth. "I forgot to tell you about Tulip."

Lexi raised an eyebrow. "You have a tulip garden? Why would that make me not want to live here?"

"No." Marina shook her head, so solemn. "My dog, Tulip."

She moved to one side and a big pink nose nudged in next to her knee. The next second, the grinning face of a huge pit bull peeked in at Lexi.

Lexi let out a little yelp of delight and instantly plopped down onto the ground, making kissing noises and holding her hand out for the dog. Tulip's nails tick-tick-ticked across the floor as she skittered over to plop onto her haunches at Lexi's side. Her pink tongue lolled to one side out of her bony skull as she sat patiently.

Lexi let the dog smell her and then traced her hands over her head and down her bony body. "Well, aren't you a beautiful girl," she cooed scratching at the gingery gold patch of fur over Tulip's right eye.

"Boy," Marina corrected. "Tulip's a boy."

Lexi let out an appreciative laugh. "Oops. I guess a dog doesn't much care what his name is, huh?"

"Can I come in?" Marina asked.

Lexi looked up, confused. "'Course."

Marina took some careful steps through the door and laid her hand on Tulip's head. Tulip instantly leaned his tremendous weight on Marina's leg.

"I renamed him Tulip when I rescued him," Marina said. "Because I know how scared people can be of pit bulls. I thought if he had a sweet name…"

"Who could be scared of this guy?" Lexi asked as she found Tulip's magic spot, the one that made his leg kick-kick-kick.

"My thoughts exactly." Marina took a deep breath. "He's a comfort dog. For me."

"Oh," Lexi snapped her hands back. "So that means I'm not supposed to touch him, right?"

"It's okay. He's not a service dog," Marina said. "I just, I struggle with anxiety and…" Another deep breath. "PTSD. And a doctor recommended that I find an animal who can help me with those feelings."

Of course, Lexi immediately wanted to ask Marina why she suffered PTSD, but she stifled the urge. She needed to earn the right to ask. Maybe they'd become friends and she could ask someday. Maybe she could even help Marina somehow. But then she reminded herself: Quicksand.

She wouldn't be here long enough to do any of that. And though that made her sad, she needed to accept it.

"Um, does Tulip leave the house with you?" she asked.

"Most of the time. He stays in the back room at the bar. Snoozing and sneaking treats from the line cooks."

Lexi grinned. "Ok, cool. Well, I don't want to step on your toes, but if you ever need somebody to let him out or walk him or something, I'm your girl. I love dogs."

"That's nice. Thank you," Marina said.

Lexi rose and realized just how much taller she was than Marina now that they were standing next to one another.

"So, uh," Lexi cleared her throat. "Thanks for letting me crash here."

"I'm grateful for the company, honestly. And for the help with the rent. This place was my father's house, before he had to go to a nursing home over in Jacksonville. And I have trouble with the mortgage some months. You hungry? I just picked up some groceries. I was going to make something before I head over to the bar."

"Sure." Lexi looked at the time on her phone. Wow. It was already almost five o'clock. The day had slipped away from her. "That sounds great."

Lexi helped Marina unpack the groceries while Tulip was belly up on the kitchen floor. Lexi couldn't help but smile every time she had to step over him. The two of them ate their sandwiches in relative silence at the breakfast bar. Lexi looking around, trying to get a feel for the house.

Marina ate slowly and methodically, then immediately stood to wash and dry her plate. "Well, I need to change and head out to the bar now," Marina said. "If you want to come by, you can have some free drinks. To celebrate your move?"

Lexi could tell the invitation, like most of what she did, made Marina nervous. She was like a pile of leaves and the world was a leaf blower. "How about tomorrow night? I want to be fresh for my first day of work tomorrow."

"Oh, right. I forgot Eric said you were working at the hardware store now."

Lexi stood, cleared her own plate and washed it. "How long have you known Eric?" she asked, trying to be casual.

"Since we were four or five. He's spent every summer here with his grandparents since around then."

"And then he'd go back to California?"

"Yup," Marina's eyes warmed. "I remember the Thanksgiving break that the boys visited him in L.A. Jake, his brother, Dean, and, um, Dylan." Her cheeks pinked at Dylan's name. "They came back with shell necklaces and sunburns and thought they could suddenly pull off words like 'gnarly' and 'radical'."

Lexi grinned. "How'd that go over in Montana?"

Marina grinned back. "Let's just say it didn't last long."

5

Eric raked his hand through his hair and fiddled with the boxes of key chains next to the cash register. He was waiting for Lexi to arrive for her first day of work at the hardware store. Why the hell was he so nervous?

They'd already slept together for fuck's sake. What was there to be nervous about? Still, he was pretty sure he'd rearranged the check-out counter five times before her car finally pulled into the parking lot.

He winced at the rattling sound of her old Honda Civic. There was no way in hell that thing could be safe. Maybe there was some way he could talk her into taking a car? A safer one? Maybe one with the hardware store logo on the side. He could tell her it was part of the employee package or something.

Yeah. Like there was any way that she would ever buy that crap. She was already half convinced that he was trying to make her into a 'kept' woman. Forcing a nicer car on her would be tantamount to buying her lingerie at this point. He was giving her a job and a little stability for the summer. That was just going to have to be enough.

His breath caught in his chest as she got out of her car then almost immediately turned and climbed back inside again.

What the hell. She was ditching?

She climbed out of her car. Walked about half-way to the front entrance. Only to turn and slink back to her car.

Eric walked to the door, ready to go after her, but then she jumped out of her car, slammed the door shut decisively and headed his way. The bell over the door dinged and she pulled up short as she saw him standing there, hands in his pockets.

They eyed one another, and Eric had to push down the impulse to close the distance between them and take her in his arms.

Shit. Maintaining a professional air between them was going to be harder than he'd anticipated.

"Hey Boss," she finally said, rocking back on her heels and tucking her hands into the pockets of her jeans. A nicer pair than she'd worn to the bar the other night.

He grimaced. "Eric's fine still."

"Sure. I, uh, wasn't sure what to wear."

He couldn't resist scanning her body, taking in her tight T-shirt, perfectly fitted jeans, and the way her hair fell all the way down to her elbows. God. Even her scuffed up Chuck Taylors were giving him a halfie. He needed to get himself under control.

Clearing his throat, Eric gestured to himself. "Jeans

are fine. It's a hardware store after all. And I have a T-shirt for you." He pointed to his own forest green company shirt, emblazoned with Iris Hardware. "Iris is my grandmother's name."

Lexi's eyes involuntarily softened. "Your grandfather named the store after her?"

"No," Eric laughed even as he strode behind the counter and pulled out her T-shirt. "She named it after herself. She's a toughie. Trust me. Takes what she wants and doesn't wait around for handouts."

"Sounds like my kind of girl," Lexi said, reaching out for the shirt and pulling it over the one she already wore.

It fit her like a glove and Eric did his best to roll his tongue back into his mouth as she flipped her glossy blonde hair out from under the collar.

"Want the grand tour?" he cleared his throat again. He was going to have to start bringing cough drops to work if they were going to be working side by side.

He showed her around the store and was pleased and relieved that she knew the names and uses of almost all the tools. He even ran a few potential customer scenarios past her and she showed a workable knowledge of how to fix all the fictional problems.

"Anything I don't know, I can just google, right?" she asked him, nodding her head at the old desktop behind the register.

"Sure, or ask me. Although, I probably won't be here most of the time."

"Alright." She ducked her head and looked out onto

the street. "Looks like you got a delivery. I'll handle it," she said and jogged out the door before he could.

Eric watched her and rubbed the back of his neck. God, he liked her. He was attracted to her. She was the hottest sex he'd ever had. Now he had to come to terms with the fact that in order to help her, he wasn't going to be able to touch her again.

Kiss her again.

Go down on her again.

Fuck her again.

Damn it! Eric groaned and reached for his cup of cooling coffee on the counter.

Lexi laughed at something the Fed Ex man said outside. Eric watched the man watch Lexi's lush ass as she bent over to pick up the package. Eric's hand tightened on the cup of coffee instead of doing what he wanted to do, which was punch the poor Fed Ex man in the face.

The bell above the door rang again and Lexi shouldered her way inside, the box in her hands.

"I'll unload this," she called to him, already tearing the tape off the box.

"You had breakfast yet?" he asked, coming around the counter.

Lexi glanced up, surprised, her eyes narrowing just a little. "Yeah. Marina made pancakes this morning and shared some with me."

Eric's eyes widened as he checked the wall clock. "Marina was up early enough to make you pancakes before work? She must have been at the bar until at least

2:30. That's less than 5 hours of sleep."

"Oh that's not good. Maybe she couldn't sleep?"

Eric's brow furrowed. He hadn't been here when things had gone south for Marina. He'd still been in L.A. And a lot of years had passed since then. She was leaps and bounds better than she used to be. Still, if she was having trouble sleeping, that wasn't a good sign. He made a mental note to check in with her. Maybe ask Dylan about it.

The bell over the door rang and distracted him from his thoughts.

"Morning, Mrs. Gunderson," he said as the older, chubby woman strode in like she owned the place. She was his grandmother's best friend and Eric knew she'd taken it upon herself to make sure he didn't run the store into the ground while Iris was on vacation.

"Mornin', boy," she said, fanning herself in the automatic gesture of a woman who knows how to weather heat the old fashioned way. "You got any more of that coffee back there?"

"Of course, ma'am." Eric tried not to sigh. He liked Mrs. Gunderson. He really did. Grew up with her as a member of the family. But getting her a cup of coffee meant she was going to stay and chat awhile. And she was infamous for having eyes like a hawk. He didn't particularly care to be observed around Lexi right now.

"Oh! Child, you scared me," Mrs. Gunderson hooted as Lexi emerged from an aisle in the store, breaking down the box she'd just finished unloading.

She stepped forward with her hand out. "Sorry about that. Lexi Fischer."

"Cheryl Gunderson." Mrs. Gunderson held Lexi's hand for just a moment while she eyed her shrewdly. "Well, aren't you an interesting creature."

Lexi raised one eyebrow at the older woman, obviously unsure what to make of her old-fashioned flower print dress, the feathered 1980s hair, or the ancient pair of cowboy boots. Or more likely, she probably wasn't sure how she felt about being called a creature.

"Not much girl in there, but pretty just the same," Mrs. Gunderson said, observing Lexi as she accepted the cup of coffee from Eric.

Lexi's eyebrow raised even further. "Uh—"

"What you know about horses, child?" Mrs. Gunderson asked as she leaned forward and squinted at one of the little silver rings that Lexi wore. Eric hadn't noticed before that it was shaped like a horse.

He shook his head at Mrs. Gunderson. Pushing 75 years old and eyes like a hawk.

Lexi straightened her shoulders and stared Mrs. Gunderson right in the eye. "I know enough."

"I suppose you learned about horses at one of them summer camps, huh? The kind with the funny hats and the polo playing."

Lexi blinked her eyes slowly and when she spoke, she was damn near matching the slow country drawl that was like syrup oozing from Mrs. Gunderson's mouth. Eric wondered if she was doing it on purpose or if it came naturally.

"No ma'am. I grew up on the rodeo circuit."

"Is that right?" She'd caught Mrs. Gunderson's attention. And Eric's. "And what was your event?"

"Ropin' and racin'. Mutton bustin' as a kid of course."

Eric tried to keep his jaw from falling open. She'd grown up in the rodeo scene? Who was this woman? And why was he starving for information about her? Everything he learned just made him want to learn more.

Now Mrs. Gunderson had a look in her eye like she was trying to swallow down a similar interest. "I did a bit of rodeo as a girl, myself." She raised her painted eyebrows. "Ain't no easy world for a woman."

Lexi shrugged. "I had my daddy there. He looked out for me."

Mrs. Gunderson surveyed her for another second. "So, you going to come by my porch and talk to me about rodeo sometime?"

"That an invitation?"

"Sure was."

"Alright then," Lexi rocked back on her heels. "I suppose I will."

"That's just fine," Mrs. Gunderson said as she pushed the half drunk cup of coffee back into Eric's hand. "But Mr. Gunderson and I are a bit formal when we have guests. Wear a dress."

Lexi's eyebrows raised and this time she was much more amused than offended. "And what if I don't have a dress to wear?"

Mrs. Gunderson didn't turn around, just kept striding toward the door. "Buy one," she threw back over her shoulder before she left.

"That is one old school lady," Lexi said, going up on her toes to watch her sway down the street. "Real country."

Eric raised his eyebrows and leaned forward, unable to resist brushing her hair back from her shoulder. "Rodeo, huh?"

She shrugged. "Everybody's gotta grow up somewhere."

* * *

Time passed easily for Lexi that day. There was a lot to learn and always something to get done. She liked being busy. Since life was all about balance, she also liked taking breaks. She'd just put her feet up in the back room when she heard the bell ring above the door.

Figured. Barely three customers all day and then the second she took a break, somebody walked in. She'd just stood when a slinky, female voice made its way into the backroom.

"Hey there, Eric."

"Afternoon, Sarah," Eric said. "You need something fixed?"

"As a matter of fact, I do," the woman replied silkily, her tone making Lexi think, *I just bet you need something fixed.*

Unable to stop herself, Lexi peeked out the slightly open door.

She immediately spotted long silky blonde hair and a sliver of a powder pink dress.

"I've got a lamp that won't turn on back home. I was wondering if you could come take a look at it."

Eric cleared his throat. "Chances are you just need a new bulb. You know what wattage you're looking for?" He started to guide the woman—*Sarah*—toward the lighting section of the store. She turned just enough for Lexi to get a load of her perfect D cup breasts.

"Well, wouldn't you know it, it's this funny little European thing that Daddy brought back from Venice for me. And I can't for the life of me figure out what kind of bulb it'll take. But I brought a picture of the lamp to show you. Maybe you can figure it out."

Eric leaned closer to look at her phone, and Lexi watched his eyebrows lift up into his hairline. "Uh, Sarah, not sure that's the picture you meant to show me."

Sarah's musical little laugh tinkled through the store, making Lexi's fingernails bite into her palms where she clenched her fists.

"Oh my," Sarah cooed. "Sorry about that." She didn't sound sorry at all. She swiped through a few pictures and Lexi could tell by the expression on Eric's face that each was more explicit than the next. "Here's the lamp."

Eric cleared his throat. "Yeah. Um follow me, we've got a few of those bulbs left in stock."

"Thank goodness," Sarah replied. "It's the lamp on

my bedside table and I really like to keep the lights on when I'm in bed… for reading."

Lexi clenched her fists. She was all for women expressing their sexuality. And as someone who'd fucked a near stranger in a barn two nights ago, she wasn't trying to slut shame. But for the love of god! This was Eric's place of work! Where a customer like Mrs. Gunderson could walk in any moment!

And even though she knew it was an utterly ridiculous thought, she couldn't help thinking of Eric as *her* man. And she certainly didn't want Sarah with her D-cup breasts and whatever-naughty-pictures she had on her phone flirting with her man.

Eric didn't say much else, just rang up her purchase, accepted the breathy little kiss on the cheek she gave him, and then let out one long breath when she trounced out the door.

Lexi leaned on the doorjamb of the break room and cleared her throat.

Eric turned to her. "Oh, hey. I suppose you saw all that?" He pointed his thumb toward the door that sweet little Sarah had just left through.

"Some of it," Lexi said, jamming her hands in her pockets. "Though it seems you're the one who got the eyeful."

"Boy, did I." Eric grimaced. "I think what she was doing in one of those pictures was technically illegal."

"And she just up and flashed them at you? Takes a lot gumption." Lexi sauntered forward, her hands still in her pockets, a neutral expression on her face.

"Takes a lot of something." He stared at her a second, tilted his head, then grinned. "You don't seem particularly shocked at the idea of naked pictures. Is that because you've taken some yourself?"

She hadn't, but instead of telling him that, she just shrugged. "It's the age of the camera phone."

Eric's mouth dropped open. "Well, damn. Show me."

Lexi pulled up short at how quickly his playful tone turned commanding. It reminded her of how dominant he'd been that night in the barn, pinning her hands to that beam. Afraid he'd see and correctly interpret the movement, she refused to press her legs together even though she desperately wanted to.

"I'm your employee, remember?"

"Fine. You're fired. Now, show me." He held his hand out for her phone, but his tone had tuned playful again, and he wore a small, friendly smile on his face.

Lexi couldn't help but smile back. "I told you we're not sleeping together again, Eric."

"That's fine, but you didn't say we couldn't flirt with each other. I *might* be able to handle not sleeping with you. But not flirting with you? You ask the impossible. That's just fighting against biology."

"Fair enough. Flirting? Fine. Fucking? Not fine."

"Fine." He grinned again, and God, he was so beautiful he was hard to look at sometimes. "And for the record, sexting, whether it comes in the form of pictures or text, counts as flirting, not fucking."

She rolled her eyes. "It certainly does not."

He opened his mouth to say something else but his phone buzzed with an incoming text. He checked it, then said, "My friend Jake wants to know if you want to come have a drink with us tonight. Maybe we can take a poll about the sexting debate. What do you say?"

Lexi stepped up to the check-out counter and fiddled with one of the key chains they sold. "Who's us?"

"Me and Jake and Dylan. And maybe our friend Will. We meet each other at the bar a few times a week."

"Skeeps?" Lexi asked, naming the bar where Marina worked.

He nodded.

"I'm already going," Lexi responded. "Marina and I are celebrating our new living arrangement."

She ignored the way his face lit up when she said that she was going to be there. It wasn't good for the little erratic pitter patter in her heart.

"That's great!"

"I'm not going to stay too long though," she warned him. "I've got work in the morning."

He smiled at her. "Me too. And a full day of flirting ahead of me."

Lexi would never admit it, but Lord, she liked the sound of that. Somehow she managed to say, "Flirt all you want. But remember sexting is *not* flirting."

Eric just laughed. "We'll see about that."

6

Eric was screwed.

Why the hell had he agreed to keep his hands off Lexi? And why the hell had he told Dylan and Jake that they'd decided to be just friends?

Jake had gotten that shit eating grin on his face as he'd watched Lexi order a drink from Marina at the bar. "So the new girl's up for grabs then?"

It had taken every ounce of self control that Eric had not to backhand Jake across his pretty, asshole face. Jesus, first the Fed Ex guy. Now Jake. Eric had never had a problem with feeling proprietary over a woman.

Not until Lexi.

Dylan had clapped a hand on Eric's shoulder. "Y'all don't look like 'just friends', but whatever you gotta tell yourself, brother."

And now they were all sitting in a booth in the back of Skeeps, Jake and Eric on one side and Dylan and Lexi on the other.

Dylan had been quietly talking with Lexi for the last twenty minutes and Eric was getting in an increasingly bad mood just watching them.

He sipped his beer and turned to Jake. "Jake," he said, loud enough for them to hear across the booth. "In your expert opinion, is sexting filed under the 'flirting' category or the 'sex' category."

Jake grinned, tipped back his baseball cap, and took a long, meditative sip of beer. "Interesting question, my dude." He squinted his eyes and seemed to look off into the distance.

Lexi's face was neutral across the table, but Eric was almost positive she was about to break into either a scowl or a smile.

"In my extremely expert opinion," Jake started. "After years of research, focus groups, test after test—"

"Jesus Christ," Dylan grumbled before taking the last swig of his beer and motioning for more from Marina.

"I would have to say that as you can't get somebody pregnant from sexting, it is firmly in the category of flirting." Jake tapped his beer on the table like a judge tapping a gavel to signal the end of court.

Eric raised an eyebrow at Lexi across the booth who raised one right back.

"Still, there are degrees of flirting, wouldn't you say?" Dylan said in his lazy drawl, eyeing Marina as she approached the table with another round for everybody. "Flirting between strangers. Flirting between friends. Flirting between people who have far more in mind.

Wouldn't you say that sexting is flirting with a definite destination?"

Marina's hands bobbled her tray before she quickly righted it. Dylan's gaze stayed fixated on her face, but she staunchly ignored him, setting the drinks down in front of everybody.

For the hundredth time in the last few days, Eric wondered what was going on between his two friends. And even though he knew she should let Marina off the hook, what with the way she was blushing, he also couldn't help but wonder if perhaps she and Dylan could have something special, if only they were given half the chance.

"What do you think, Marina?" he asked her. "Is sexting just flirting?"

She pursed her lips. "I wouldn't know."

Jake leaned back in his seat. "You've never sexted anybody before?"

"I…" Marina's cheeks flamed as she stared resolutely at the table. "I, well, I guess I'm not sure how you'd define sexting."

"Well," Jake said, "sexting is defined as one, naked pictures; two, dirty words; three—"

"Intentionally trying to get the person you're texting all worked up," Dylan cut in.

Marina's cheeks flamed even harder before she narrowed her eyes at Dylan and raised her chin. "Well I guess maybe I have sexted before."

"So, what do you think? Is sexting just harmless

flirting?" Eric asked again.

"Flirting is never harmless if it could ruin a friendship," Marina answered, tucking her empty tray under her arm and hurrying back toward the safety of the bar.

"I guess the jury's still out on that one," Lexi muttered as she watched Marina's retreating back. A tense silence came over the table. Suddenly, Dylan cursed. When he slid out of the booth to go after her, Lexi suddenly pressed a hand to his arm, stopping him.

"Do you mind if I talk to her?" she asked.

Dylan opened his mouth to argue, his eyes flitting back to Marina. Then he glanced at Eric.

Eric nodded. "You can trust Lexi. I do."

With that, Dylan reluctantly settled back into the booth.

Lexi mouthed, "Thank you," then headed after Marina.

* * *

Lexi patted Tulip on his big, grinning skull as soon as she entered the backroom where Marina was sitting on a case of bottled water in the back corner.

"Hey, girl," Lexi said, turning over a bucket to sit on and taking a seat next to her. "Look, I know we don't know one another very well. And subtlety isn't exactly my strong suit. But I don't ever lie and I don't ever tell secrets. So, if you want to talk about it, whatever *it* was out there, the buck stops with me."

Marina took a deep breath and immediately Tulip was there, pushing his head under her hand and letting his tongue loll to one side. "I don't know what the hell that was either. I..." She took another deep breath. "I was happy being just friends, you know. I don't need a man. I don't *want* one. Not after..."

Lexi gently laid a hand on Tulip's head. Marina's eye followed Lexi's movements like a bird following a fly swatter. It made something bone deep and awful cry out inside Lexi. It was obvious someone had hurt Marina and once again, Lexi wanted to ask, but Marina was trembling like the last leaf on a branch and Lexi didn't want to tip her over the edge.

"You don't have to tell me everything but just to tell me about one thing, Marina," Lexi said softly. "Tell me about Dylan."

Marina sighed softly and Lexi wondered if she knew how much longing was in that sound. "We've been friends our whole lives. And actually, he was the one who saved me from... something really bad. The worst thing that's ever happened to me. And since then, he's been my *best* friend. But lately, he wants more than I can give."

"Maybe you just *think* you can't give more," Lexi said.

Marina looked into Lexi's eyes and gave her the most solid, direct look that she'd seen from her yet. "No. That part of me is dead. It has been for a long time. And Dylan looking all handsome and talking all sweet and coming around with rides home and texting me when he thinks about me… He's trying to resurrect something that's better off dead. And it's causing me to do things. Things I shouldn't do, that just give him false hope…"

"Well," Lexi said, scratching Tulip under his chin. "If you don't want him, you don't want him. And that's something he better come to terms with quick."

Marina winced. "It's not that easy. Sometimes you can want something and just have to accept you can't have it. No matter how much you wish things were different. Sometimes we have to make the difficult choice and live by that choice. Do you know what I mean?"

Lexi stared at Marina, thinking of the choice she'd made to keep her heart safe from Eric, then nodded. "Yes, I know what you mean." She wished she didn't. She wished she could contradict Marina and tell her that no matter what happened in the past, she didn't have to deprive herself of what could make her happy in the present. But that would be hypocritical on Lexi's part. She knew all about having to make the difficult choice. In Lexi's case, the difficult choice was to avoid any emotional ties that would get in the way with her dreams. In Marina's case? If she wanted to choose feelings of safety and piece-of-mind over what Dylan could give her, then who was Lexi to argue with her?

Marina suddenly stood. "I should get back out there. But Lexi?"

Lexi looked up at her new friend. "Yes?"

"You and Eric. I…sense something between the two

of you. And I want you to know, the same's true with me. If you ever want to talk, the buck stops here."

Lexi smiled. "Thank you, Marina."

Marina left and for a moment, Lexi just sat there. Then she followed Marina out to the bar, stopping to order a glass of water to bring back to the table.

When her phone buzzed in her pocket, she knew immediately who was texting her.

She bit her lip and replayed all that had just happened. She'd made her difficult choice.

She had, but she also wasn't Marina. She didn't have to draw such hard lines when it came to her attraction to a handsome man who clearly wanted her.

No, she couldn't have Eric, not without risking her dreams of moving to L.A. and becoming a screenwriter. But so long as she didn't get too involved, as long as she didn't sleep with him again, would it really be so bad to continue enjoying some harmless flirting? After all, she hadn't been hurt, not like Marina. She was thinking far more clearly. And Eric knew exactly how things were. That she wasn't staying. That the last thing she wanted was quicksand.

So...

Unable to resist, she slid her phone out of her pocket and sure enough, there was a text from Eric.

-See? Even Marina sexts. And she was a band geek in high school.

Lexi couldn't help but laugh. She turned and flashed a smile over her shoulder at Eric. He sat with one arm over the back of the booth, talking with Dylan, but her smile caught his eye and pretty soon he was grinning and shrugging right back at her.

Lexi faced back toward the bar in time to see Marina sliding over a bright red drink with a little sprig of green poking out of it. Lexi raised an eyebrow and tossed some of her hair back over her shoulder.

"I know I look like a total girly girl," Lexi joked, "but I draw the line at fruity drinks."

"Trust me," Marina responded easily. "This isn't too girly. I made it up. It's hibiscus, rosemary iced tea with vodka and just a kiss of lime. Not sweet at all."

With one eyebrow still raised, Lexi leaned in and took a sip. The flavor exploded in her mouth. "Holy shit, Mari."

Marina grinned. "Told ya."

"Fuck Dylan," Lexi said, taking another drink. "You're my girlfriend now."

For a second, Lexi bit her tongue, worrying that she'd gone too far, but Marina only laughed. A little delighted sound. She moved down the bar to take another patron's order and Lexi found herself eyeing her phone again.

Either it was the vodka in the drink or Lexi was really trying to walk the walk, but she took a deep breath. Honesty time.

-Flirting/sexting sounds fun. But it also sounds like another word for quicksand.

Instantly, the dots that meant he was typing a reply showed up on the screen, and Lexi swallowed down the little giddy bubble that had risen in her chest.

-Not quicksand. I promise. Consider it practice for your first few lonely weeks in L.A. You're going to need SOMEBODY to take care of those needs. And by then I'll be a thousand miles away. Nobody can get stuck in quicksand from a thousand miles away.

Lexi sucked her teeth and tried not to smile. It all came down to how much she trusted herself and Eric. Did she trust Eric to help her chase her dream at the end of the summer? Did she trust herself to know what she was doing?

Lexi signaled to Marina that she was heading for the bathroom. Flipping the lock, Lexi debated taking a picture in the mirror, classic selfie-style, but she instead held the phone over her head. She looked up at the camera, making sure that the lens got a great view right down her top. She leaned forward just a little, her breasts, which were on the larger side, crushed against her bra. At the last second, Lexi brought her thumb up to her bottom lip, pulled it just slightly down, and snapped the picture. She turned around her camera to see the image.

Bingo.

She looked sexy, turned on, and all kinds of bothered. She scuttled back out of the bathroom and sat on a bar stool. Tossing her hair behind her back, she took another long sip of her drink and pulled open her text convo with Eric.

And she sent the photo.

She couldn't help but grin when she heard him coughing up a swallow of his beer behind her. Mission accomplished.

And then her phone buzzing with his reply.

J

E

S

U

S

C

H

R

I

S

T

-You gotta warn a man, woman!

Lexi couldn't help but grin.

-You got what you wanted and now you're complaining?

-Hell no, not complaining. I'm in the process of bowing down to my new god. Well, Gods, I should say. Your breasts deserve a house of worship.

Lexi rolled her eyes.

-Your turn, she texted.

-To send a pic?

-Duh.

Within seconds, he was at her elbow at the bar, but he didn't speak to her. "Marina! Another round for the boys, alright? My tab."

He didn't look back at her as he walked down the back hall.

Lexi picked up her phone. She needed to clarify one thing.

-No dick pics.

She heard his bark of laughter as he stepped into the bathroom and closed the door.

Seconds later she received a picture he'd taken of his reflection in the bathroom mirror. It showed him with one hand pulling up his shirt, revealing his six pack abs and the v of his muscles down into the waistband of his pants. The band of his briefs hung dangerously low on his hips.

Lexi's mouth went dry. God he was so hot. And his face.

She stifled a groan. He wasn't smoldering cheesily for the camera like guys so often did in sexy pics.

No, he was just smiling, but there was a definite message in his eyes. One that said he wanted to lick her from head to toe.

Lexi took a deep breath and another sip of her drink. When Eric emerged from the bathroom, Lexi lifted her glass and toasted him.

He winked and took a little bow.

Flirting, she told herself. Just some harmless flirting.

But even as the words echoed in her head, the fluttery feeling in her stomach—and in her heart—gave her pause. And made her wonder if of the two of them, Marina wasn't the smart one, after all.

7

Eric and Lexi fell into a rhythm. A very sexy, thrilling rhythm, but a rhythm nonetheless. Work during the days, where they kept things professional. The bar during the nights, where they let themselves flirt, but only so far. A few days turned into a week and then a week turned into two.

It was at the end of her second week working at the hardware store that Lexi got her first check, and she immediately sent half the money to her father. But more than the money, she was enjoying herself. Work was fun, even more fun when Eric was around. The only times that weren't so fun were when Miss Sarah Burn flounced her ass into the store and fawned all over Eric.

And unfortunately, right now was one of those times.

Eric was leading Sarah around the store, adding this and that to her cart. She was pretty sure that he was trying to hurry her out of there, but even that was annoying to Lexi right now.

After Sarah dropped $125 on crap Lexi was sure she didn't need, she kissed Eric on the cheek and left. Lexi tried biting back her thoughts, but it was no use. She said, "I'll bet all her panties match her bras."

"Excuse me?" Eric said, one eyebrow raised, freezing in the act of hauling some seasonal items back toward the back room.

"You heard me. I'll bet she never uses her toothbrush after the blue stripe is gone. That Daddy carves the thanksgiving turkey and someday, hubby will. But she'll be too busy licking her lips at the pool boy to notice."

"Wow." Eric grabbed a broom from the back room and started sweeping up. "That's quite the story you've spun there." He paused. "Freaky accurate, too."

"It's a gift." Lexi shrugged, marked two things off her inventory list. "I can make up a backstory for anybody I meet."

"Anybody, huh? What about Mrs. Gunderson?" he challenged her.

"Well, that's sort of cheating because she already told me about her rodeo days, but sure. I can fill in the rest." Lexi leaned back and thought for a second. "Her daddy was a rich man, owned a mine, maybe. But the mine caved in and the money dried up. She had to learn how to bring home the bacon fast. She was young, pretty, and could ride a horse. She joined the circuit. She was good, but too feisty, the men wanted her and she wanted to be left alone. She quit, moved north, did something boring for a few years, just long enough to meet Mr. Gunderson. Sweet, calm, steady. He didn't have much, but he knew how to work. Which in Mrs. Gunderson's book, meant a hell of a lot more. They tried to have kids, couldn't. So she made the town her baby. And she's a bit of an overbearing mama. She likes to know who, what, when, where, and how. And for her, that's enough."

Eric's mouth had dropped dead open. "Not far off, actually. I'm pretty sure her father owned a ranch that went under, not a mine. But your version's more interesting."

"Storyteller," she pointed at herself. "I can make anybody's life into a movie. Except for mine."

"Anybody's?"

She shrugged again. "Try me."

"What about mine?"

Lexi put one hand on her hip and cocked her head while Eric dumped the contents of the dustpan into the trash and locked the front door of the hardware store, flipping the sign from open to closed.

"Hmmm…Well, Eric, I'd say you come from money." She squinted her eyes at him. "Yeah, definitely. But it motivated you, not made you lazy. You have a good relationship with your parents. Closer to your mom than your dad. No brothers or sisters. Lately though, you've grown suspicious of the people in your rich bitch circle. You never know who wants you or your cash. You've come back here in search of the simple life. And you're surprised at how easy it was to make the switch. It was hard to leave your folks behind but you didn't have any close friends, never really had a girl who meant anything much to you, so you packed up and…"

Lexi's voice trailed off as something dark flashed over Eric's face. Something that looked an awful lot like pain.

He took a step backward and flipped off the lights in the store. Then he walked toward her in the dim light. "Wow, you're pretty good," he said in a tight voice.

"Eric," she said quietly, hurrying around the counter toward him. "I was just messing around. Stabs in the dark. I didn't mean—"

"No, no. You were mostly right. Except for a few things. I'm equally close to my parents. And it wasn't easy to leave my life in L.A. To come here. It was terribly tough, actually. I left behind my best friend in the world and a girl I'd loved for six years." He turned to her and the dim light filtered over his face. "Don't think they've missed me much though. And if they did, they have one another for comfort."

She'd never seen him look like this. If it were anyone else, she would have thought that she saw rage in his expression. But not Eric. No. It was disappointment in himself that she saw on his face.

"Oh, Eric." Unable to do anything else, she closed the distance between them, and banded her arms around his waist tightly. "I'm so sorry I said those things. I don't know why—"

"No, it's ok. You didn't know." He traced a hand over her hair and Lexi almost went weak with relief that he wasn't pushing her away. "It just hit me, you know?

Here's Lexi, this woman who I think knows me pretty well already, and she's telling me that I come off like I've never really loved anybody. And it just made me wonder what it is about me that reads that way. You know, was it the same thing that made Brianne turn to Gabe? Is there something about me that shuts people out?"

"No!" Lexi shook her head from side to side, staring up at him. "No, that's not why I said that. You make it sound like it's because you're cold or unloving or something, but really it's the opposite."

"What do you mean?" He tried to take a step back from her, but Lexi refused to let go.

"I said what I said because you're so warm. So loyal. So passionate. So…pure. I just thought that if you'd really loved somebody, it would have left a mark that showed forever. But just because I didn't see it, doesn't mean that it wasn't there. I'm so sorry—"

"You think I'm those things? Warm? Loyal? Pure?"

"Are you nuts? Of course! Dylan and Jake would lay down on train tracks for you. You're the only one who loosens Marina up. Everybody lights right up when you're around."

"And passionate?"

Lexi held his gaze. Her stomach flipped and she felt a warm feeling of relief slide through her veins. He was getting a certain look in his eye that was telling her he wasn't quite as hurt as he'd been a few minutes ago. "Of course passionate. I was there that night in the barn, remember? You're skilled and hot and considerate." She licked her lips. "Creative. You made me… react in a way I never had before. Lit me up."

"Lit you up?" he asked, his eyes dropping to her lips where she traced her tongue over her bottom lip once more.

"Like a birthday cake with a hundred candles. And then when I couldn't take it anymore, you blew me right out."

Suddenly, Lexi was very aware that they were standing in a dark room, completely alone, and she was still holding him around his waist like she was terrified he might get away. Her breasts were smashed into his hard chest, which was made all the more obvious by her panting breaths.

"I was rougher with you than I usually am. More…demanding," he said, so close that she could feel his breath on her lips.

She was dimly aware that he was walking her backward. That there were shelves at her back. He planted a hand on either side of her head, looked down at her with some unnamed emotion in his eyes.

"Did you hear me complaining?"

He stilled. Studied her face for a moment, his body like warm steel underneath her hands. A small smile softened his face for just a moment. "You liked it."

She bit her lip and nodded. Found she couldn't lie to him. "Yes."

"You liked when I made you grab that beam." He leaned down just a touch further. "When I made you come on my mouth. When I bent you over and took you from behind."

"Yes," she gulped, frozen, in his thrall. She knew there were reasons she'd avoided moments like this with him, but she couldn't for the life of her remember them. Her life didn't exist outside this room. All she had were these four walls and this hulking sex god leaning over her.

"You liked it when I fucked you on your hands and knees."

"Yes," she gasped, so aware of him surrounding her in every way. His hands on either side of her head. His strong body filling up all the space in front of her.

And then there was no more space between them. His mouth dropped to hers and she was swallowing down his kisses, moaning into his mouth. Lexi's hands finally unwound from around his waist but only to tangle into his hair. She knew she was tugging at him too tight, but he only groaned and pushed her farther into the shelves behind her.

The last two weeks of abstaining from one another's bodies had taken its toll. Every moment where she'd wanted to touch him and barely managed to stop herself was piling up and tearing out of her. Lexi moaned as her head fell back.

Eric lowered his mouth to her neck, sucking and nibbling at the exposed skin there.

Before she knew it, her legs were up around his waist and he was spinning away from the shelves, striding toward their little break room table where Lexi ate lunch everyday. Eric reached out with one hand and yanked the tablecloth, sending all the odds and ends on the table bouncing to the floor.

And then Lexi was spread out before him on the table.

* * *

Lexi was everything he'd ever wanted.

No, she was everything he *needed* right here and now.

Nothing more, nothing less.

Because that was all she could give him—this moment—so that was all he was going to take.

But he sure as fuck was going to take it.

With a few tight movements, he undid her jeans.

He tossed one of her shoes to the side and then the other.

And then he ripped her pants away.

Eric groaned at the sight of her blue cotton panties. Nothing fancy. Vaguely boyish. Sexy as fuck. Just perfectly Lexi. He grasped one of her knees and then the other. Leaning forward, he nipped her just hard enough on the inside of one of her thighs to make her gasp.

His eyes bore into hers. "Tell me you want this, Lexi."

"I do," she gasped, working her hips in the air as if she were searching for a release. "Please."

"Please what?" Eric asked, devilishly tilting his head to one side.

He expected to see annoyance or frustration on her face; instead, all he saw was her need. Her willingness to submit to him. How much she wanted it.

"Please make me come."

He didn't waste another second. Yanking her panties to one side, Eric leaned in and devoured her. She was just as sweet as she'd been before. She was tight liquid heat on his tongue and he was addicted to her. He took his time, but when she began to whimper, plant her feet on the table underneath her, whip her head from side to side, Eric changed gear. He suckled at her clit, circling it and then soothing with the flat of his tongue when the sensations got to be too much. Lexi's back arched, her fingers digging into the edge of the table.

Eric reached up and grabbed one of her hands, tangling it in his own hair so that she'd have something to anchor herself to.

She yanked and the bite of pain had Eric grinning, growling, and ruthlessly fucking her with his mouth. And when she was close, so close that she was trembling, Eric pulled away.

It was painful for him, physically painful to deny her, but he wanted, needed, to be inside her when she came. She whimpered at the loss of him, holding out one hand and giving him those eyes. Those eyes that nearly brought him to his knees, dark, lost in passion, needing.

The way she was looking at him, reaching for him, made him feel ten feet tall. He wanted to reward her for it. Make her come so hard she would never regret being with him.

Eric ripped off his belt and when it came through the

last loops, the leather snapped against itself, the sound ringing out in the quiet room.

Lexi's eyes blazed and her nostrils flared. She licked her lips and her expression grew ravenous.

Note. Taken.

But not now. He tossed the belt aside and then shoved his pants down to his knees, his cock springing free. Eric found he only had the patience to slick the condom on. His pants and shoes were just going to have to hang on for the ride. Lexi's eyes flared again. Just at the sight of him looming over her, cock hard and straining for her.

He climbed on the table, kneeled in front of her, and immediately dragged one of her legs over his shoulder, opening her up to him. It took everything he had not to plunge into her right there.

"Eric," she whispered.

But her words fell away when his fingers found her core. He pulled her panties to one side and stroked and petted her, lost in the sight of his thick digits disappearing inside her. And when he'd stoked the fire again, brought her to within a whisper of the edge, Eric gripped her hips, tipped her up, and fed himself into her. Inch by torturous inch.

Lexi's back arched completely off the table, her mouth falling open and her eyes wide and unseeing. Her pussy clenched in orgasm, and he prolonged it for her as best as he could, circling her clit with his thumb and pushing inexorably forward with his cock, giving her just enough friction to keep her coming.

Finally, her body fell lax and she went limp as a willow tree.

"Eric," she whispered again.

"I'm right here, sweetheart," he told her, holding her still against him. "I've got you. I've got you." And then he pulled out, just enough to plunge back in.

She came alive under him. Her fingers clawed at his back, leaving marks even through his shirt. Her leg slipped from his shoulder and joined the other one around his waist. Her tongue found his inside his mouth and pushed, warred, took.

Eric found their rhythm, a full, relentless beat that shook the table underneath them and sent them both soaring. He tore his mouth away from hers and groaned. She felt too good. She was destroying him. Even though he was on top, she was taking him apart, stroke by stroke. He was torn between wanting to rise up and watch her and wanting to fall further down and feel her. He wanted both. He wanted it all.

Where Lexi was concerned, he wanted everything.

It was that terrifying thought that had him pressing himself harder into her. Because all they had was this moment. There was no future for them. Which meant that Eric had to get everything he needed out of this. And he had to give her everything she needed. He nestled his face in the crook where neck met shoulder and breathed in her scent. So clean, so simple. It drove him wild. He thrust and thrust into her, and Lexi clutched him close, grinding her hips against him, moans of pleasure escaping her lips.

"Come on my cock," he growled at her looking down to where they were joined. "Show me."

Lexi immediately followed directions, thrusting her hips up. "Oh god," she half moaned, half screamed as her eyes glazed over. She pressed herself to him over and over, fucking him from below. God, he didn't know how much more he could take. He buried his face into the crook of her shoulder again and rode her, hard. Each stroke pushed him further and further into the unknown.

Suddenly, she came again, convulsing around him and screaming his name. In that moment, he felt as if they could spiral off into nothingness, so he opened his mouth and clamped down on her. One hand twisted around her back and gripped her opposite shoulder. His other hand did the same for her hips. He clasped her to him in every way possible when he came.

And came. And came.

* * *

"Holy fuck," Lexi gasped, brushing the sweaty hair off her forehead. She'd gripped his back so hard that her fingers were stiff.

"I'll move," Eric gasped. "Just gimme one—"

"Holy fuck," Lexi said again.

They couldn't help the rising laughter that came through them, shook them against each other and reminded them that Eric had yet to pull out.

"Alright, alright," Eric muttered into her neck and

reached down to take care of the condom. He slid off of her, tossed the condom in the trash and pulled up his pants. He rooted around on the ground for her pants for a second, gave up and just joined her again on the table. He collapsed again, but this time with just his head on her chest instead of his whole weight.

The action both warmed and terrified her. She hadn't wanted him to just get right up and get dressed and walk out. But this sweet version of him, nuzzling at her breasts through her shirt, humming in contentment as their legs tangled, well it was just plain dangerous. Lexi felt the ground tilt under her. He was changing the playing field.

Quicksand.

Panic rose in her throat, gripped at her chest, and she swallowed hard against it. This was not the time to freak out. So they'd had sex again. Just because it had been the most passionate, tuned in, rewarding sex she'd ever had in her life, that didn't have to mean anything.

Well, of course it meant something. It just didn't have to mean *everything*.

She and Eric were compatible. That was all. They were two compatible people who had come to know a little more about one another and liked what they were learning.

"You freaking out over there?" Eric asked, raising his head and smiling and looking more handsome than anyone had a right to. God. He was not making this easy on her.

"No," she answered too quickly. "Why would I be?"

He smirked, like he knew exactly how much she was lying. "Quicksand."

She eyed him suspiciously. "Are you trying to quicksand me?"

"No," he answered easily, propping himself up on one hand. "I just figured you'd put what we just did in the quicksand category."

She could either freak out and make this into a big, sticky mess. Or she could take it on the chin, like a big girl, and handle it. "Sorry, but that wasn't quicksand sex." Liar!

He raised his eyebrows and looked mildly scandalized. She laughed and quickly corrected herself. "Trust me, that was hot sex. Deeply hot sex. Like the best sex ever actually." His face resumed a much less offended expression. "But that wasn't quicksand sex."

He opened his mouth, like he wanted to say more, but then he shrugged, stood up and reached a hand out for her. "Whatever you say, boss."

Lexi smiled tightly as she sat up, the weight of her lies silently mocking her. "You're the boss, not me," she somehow managed to say.

He reached down for her pants and helped her into them, one leg at a time. Then he helped her put on her socks and shoes. Lexi staunchly ignored the fluttering in her stomach at the sweetness of the act. Hot sex, she reminded herself. Passionate even. But this was not love.

Love was instant quicksand.

Still kneeling in front of her, Eric's eyes bored into hers. "Lexi, when it comes to this, you're the boss."

"Deciding the rules around having sex?" she asked

quietly, needing to understand.

"Yes," he answered, rising and giving her a hand off the table. "You have needs and rules around what we can and can't do before you leave. And I totally get it. You want a clean break in August. You deserve a clean break in August. But if it were up to me, I'd have you in my bed every night for the rest of the summer."

Lexi slowly inhaled and exhaled. "Um..."

"I don't say that to pressure you. At all. Really. I just want you to know where I stand. With you, I'm going to take what I can get, okay?"

She nodded. "Fair enough."

She was relieved that her legs were holding her up, that her breath was returning to normal. But her mind was absolutely racing.

Eric's phone dinged and he checked the text. "Do you want to join me and the gang at the old drive-in for a movie night?"

Don't do it, she thought. Don't spend any more time with him, not now. Not after what just happened. That's what her head was telling her was smart. But as was often the case whenever she was around Eric, Lexi didn't do what she knew was smart. She did what came naturally.

Eric and movies were two of her favorite things. She couldn't pass up the chance to combine them in one special night. August was coming, and that meant so was the end of their time together. And just maybe...

Well, Lexi was definitely going to consider what Eric said, about him wanting her in his bed for the summer, even with the knowledge that she'd be leaving for L.A. soon.

Lexi reached into her pocket and pulled out her phone. "Let me text Marina, it's her night off tonight. Maybe we can all go. What time should we meet you there?"

"I can pick you up at Marina's in about an hour?"

"Great!" She turned on her heel and was marching out of the back room before she stopped and turned back to him. She pointed at the table where he'd just fucked her silly. "I hope you'll be using that as evidence that you're everything I said you were, Eric. Warm. Loyal. And passionate. Definitely passionate."

He grinned, walked toward her, pulled her into his arms, and kissed her deeply. Lexi felt herself lift, ever so slightly, off the earth.

Finally, he pulled away, kissed her on the nose, and patted her ass. "See you in an hour, Lex."

8

"Are you sure I won't be crashing your date?" Marina asked for the eighty millionth time as she fretted in front of her closet, looking for something to wear.

Lexi was sprawled on the floor of Marina's bedroom, petting Tulip along his back, scratching him under his chin. "One, you're specifically invited. Two, Jake's going to be there too, so you won't be a third wheel. And three, Eric and I aren't dating. So it is impossible for you to be crashing a date between us."

Marina turned, a beige sweater in one hand and a gray sweater in the other. "Not dating?" she asked with a sly look on her face. "Is that why you came home with sex hair and a bite mark on your shoulder?"

Lexi's mouth dropped open. "What are you talking about?" She scrambled up and eyed herself in Marina's bedroom mirror, yanking the collar of her shirt to one side. "Well I'll be damned."

There it was, a deliciously purple set of teeth marks right above her collar bone. Lexi ran her fingers over the mark and couldn't help the shiver that raced through her.

"For the record, this isn't evidence that we're dating." Lexi paced over to Marina, took both of the boring sweaters out of her hands and tossed them into the hamper. She started pawing through her closet, looking for something mildly interesting for her friend to wear.

"You're just fooling around then?"

Lexi huffed out a breath. "Well, we've fooled around a few times. And we're friends. That's about it."

"Are you going to do it again?" Marina asked.

Lexi wasn't usually big on sharing this kind of information with people. But there was something about the way that Marina was asking. She wasn't asking to get the dirty details. She was asking because she didn't understand. Because she really wanted to know how these things worked.

"I want to," Lexi admitted. "But I also know it's not a great idea."

"Why?" Marina asked, leaning against the door jamb of the closet, watching as Lexi dismissed almost every piece of clothing she owned. "Eric's such a good guy."

"Exactly," Lexi agreed. "He's so good that if I get in too deep with him I might not be able to get back out."

"You're afraid you won't want to leave in August," Marina guessed, hitting the nail on the head. "Is it possible to keep doing what you're doing with him and not get too wrapped up in it?"

Lexi turned to her, intrigued. Something told Lexi that Marina was definitely asking this question because she was trying to find similar answers for herself. Despite Marina's determination to call a halt to anything that was happening between her and Dylan, was she reconsidering? "Do you mean is it possible to have sex without falling in love or wanting more with that person?"

Marina nodded, her eyes wide and slightly embarrassed.

Lexi shrugged and turned back to the clothes. "Sure. I mean, I've been doing it for pretty much my entire sex life."

"So why can't you do that with Eric? Have sex and still keep a part of yourself closed off."

Lexi considered. "I think that gets harder when the sex is really good, you know? And the sex with Eric is really, really good." Understatement of the year, there. "It's so good in fact.." Lexi hesitated, then decided to be honest even as she continued to inspect Marina's clothing. "You have a point, Mari. And to be honest, it's something I've been asking myself. That maybe I can keep sleeping with Eric this summer as long as it didn't get too, I don't know what word I'm looking for… Too soft?"

Lexi turned to Marina, a pile of clothes in her hands.

"Um. Maybe?" Marina said. "You think that's possible?"

"Yeah," Lexi said, considering her answer and shoving a little purple T-shirt into Marina's hands along with some cut off jean shorts she'd found shoved in a drawer. "He knows how I feel. And we've already set ground rules. Maybe we just need to set a few more."

"What kind of ground rules?" Marina asked and then looked down at the clothes Lexi had chosen for her. "I can't wear these. This shirt is so small I only wear it when I'm cleaning the house and these daisy dukes were for a Halloween costume."

Lexi ignored her friend's protests about the clothes. "I'm not sure of the additional ground rules. I guess we'll have to come up with them between the two of us." Something black and silky caught her eye. "Marina, why do you have an evening gown like this?"

It was beautiful, perfectly tailored and sexy as hell. It must have cost a fortune.

Marina's face went bright red. "I bought it for a... fancy event. But I chickened out and never ended up making it inside."

Something on Marina's face told Lexi that this wasn't the time to push. So she patted Tulip on the head, stepped out of the closet and went to change her own clothes. "The boys will be here in twenty minutes."

9

As Jake drove his old pickup truck, Eric beside him and Dylan in the back set, Eric tried to ignore the feelings rising in his chest. His body was deeply sated from the incredible sex earlier. But his heart was beating like a damn jackrabbit. All because he was ten minutes away from seeing Lexi again.

Jesus, he needed to get his shit together.

Lexi had made it clear on countless occasions that they were not dating. That they were nothing more than friends. And just because they'd had sex on two occasions didn't mean—

Eric's phone buzzed in his pocket and his heart leaped when he saw it was a text from Lexi.

-I'm considering doing it again.

-Doing what?

-Letting you fuck my brains out.

Eric let out a long thin breath.

-Oh yeah? Great, really clever answer. She was just

going to fall into his arms now. He rolled his eyes at himself.

-Yeah. But with a few ground rules.

-Quicksand protection?

-Bingo.

-Alright. So what are these rules?

-No beds, for sex or sleeping together. No goo goo eyes. No acting like a couple.

Her rules simultaneously aroused and irritated him. But he wasn't about to look a gift horse in the mouth.

-Done.

By then they were pulling up to the house and she and Marina were already waiting on the front porch. He watched Lexi read his last text. She looked up and caught him in the bright dark burn of her eyes. She nodded once. And Eric couldn't help but feel like his fate had just been sealed.

The girls slid into the backseat, with Marina sandwiched between Lexi and Dylan.

"You look nice," Dylan said in a low voice to Marina.

Marina went bright red. "Lexi made me wear it."

"You can expect a thank you card in the mail sometime in the next three to five business days, Lexi."

Lexi caught Eric's eye in the rear view mirror and the two of them grinned.

Just a few minutes later, they were pulling into the drive-in and Eric could sense Lexi's excitement from half a car away.

"Ah!" she exclaimed the second she saw the big board

telling what movies they were playing. "Silverado!? That's one of my favorite westerns EVER!"

Eric puffed out his chest. Weirdly proud of himself even though this whole thing was Jake's idea. But still. He was really glad he got to be part of Lexi's happiness right now.

Jake pulled the truck into the spot backwards. "There's cushions and such in the back. Though I wasn't expecting quite so many people. We're going to have to get comfortable, y'all."

His grin was large and infectious. They were all smiling at one another as they climbed into the bed of Jake's truck, the movie screen splayed out in front of them. The men went to get refreshments and the women stayed behind to get the cushions and blankets all set up.

About two steps away from the truck, a redhead strolled past and Jake was gone, already dissolving into the crowd and talking pretty in her ear. Eric couldn't help but roll his eyes and smile as he made his way to the concessions.

Dylan jammed his hands in his pockets and strolled alongside Eric. "You've got a little bit of a shine going for her, huh?"

Eric ran a hand through his hair and weaved his way through the crowd. He considered lying. But to what end? Sure, he wished that Lexi were a bit more into the idea of actually dating him. Given his history, he was amazed he felt that way, so certain that if he had the green light, he wouldn't hesitate to get involved with Lexi even after all that had happened with Gabe and Brianne. But it had been a year, and Eric had obviously healed enough that he could recognize a good woman when he saw one. It was nothing to be ashamed of.

He sighed. "Sure seems that way. She's pretty great."

"You're together?" Dylan asked.

Eric shrugged. "For now, at least. She's leaving in August, and it's an expiration date she's been very clear about."

Dylan furrowed his brow. "How's that work, then?"

Eric wasn't sure if his friend was being purposefully obtuse or if the situation was really just that confusing. "We're hooking up for the summer is how it works."

"Alright." Dylan raised his hands in surrender, obviously not looking for a fight.

Eric took a few more steps. And couldn't help himself. "Why do you sound so skeptical about it? People hook up temporarily all the time."

"Sure, Eric." Dylan scraped a hand over his jaw as they got in line at concessions. "But not when they're looking at each other the way you two do. And I know you. You're a one-night stand or a committed-relationship kind of guy. I've never known you to find something in between."

Eric's annoyance with his friend immediately flagged. Dylan knew him very well. And he was well-meaning. Skeptical in the best way.

"You're not wrong, D. But she's moving to L.A. in August. And it's her dream. The kind that she's gotta make work or else she loses a part of herself. You think I'm going to get in the way of that?"

Dylan's eyes searched Eric's. "Dreams can change, Eric. Look at yours."

Eric laughed hollowly. "Dylan, for somebody who had to fight and scrape for every last penny he had, you sure are kind to the poor little rich boy."

Dylan brows rose. "You're saying that your dreams had the luxury of changing because you're rich?"

Eric shrugged his shoulders. "Of course. I had an entire life that I just up and left. I had my year off and now I'm moving on to ranching. If it doesn't work out, I'll be bummed, frustrated, embarrassed. Not destitute. But Lexi… well, if L.A. doesn't work out for her, she doesn't have anything else left in the basket. This is her whole life she's putting on the line here. Who am I to get in the way of that just because I happen to really, really like her? Just because it makes me sick to think about her leaving in August? I could never do that to her. That would be beyond selfish. Unforgivable."

Dylan's eyes flickered at something over Eric's shoulder and he almost imperceptibly shook his head, just once. Eric looked back but saw nothing, just the swirl of the crowd behind him.

"You ever think you're making this harder than it has to be?" Dylan asked quietly.

"You want to talk about making things stupid hard with girls we want to be with?" Eric challenged. "Because I'm pretty sure you wrote the damn book on that one."

Dylan's eyes flared for a second, first in anger and then in humor. He raised and dropped his shoulders. "Fair enough."

"Look," Eric said, with enough resignation in his eyes to get his friend's eyes furrowing. "It's not my first choice here. But it's the one I've been given. Take it or leave it, she says. So, what am I going to do? Not be with her at all? Watch her be with somebody else? Nah. Pass. Hard pass."

"I understand that, my brother." Dylan passed a hand over his eyes. "Jesus, do I understand that."

Eric surveyed Dylan as they came up to the front of the concessions line. "Five beers, five hotdogs with the works, five pretzels, five waters, and three large popcorns." He turned to Dylan. "So you ever going to tell me what the hell is going on with you and Marina?"

Dylan opened his mouth. Clapped it back closed.

"It might help, dude," Eric said, sliding money over the counter and easily accepting the cash that Dylan shoved in his hand. Just because he was a billionaire didn't mean his friends liked it when he paid for everything. "Seriously. Talking about it makes it less confusing sometimes."

Eric accepted the change and Dylan started loading up a tray with all the junk that Eric had ordered. "I don't know, man." He glanced around at the crowd as if he were trying to make sure they were alone. "Some days she's like a little lost kitten. And some days she's like a tiger. I never know what I'm going to get."

121

Eric took the second tray and they started back through the crowd. "She's been through a lot. I imagine that she's had to develop a few different skill sets to get back to herself."

"Sure," Dylan nodded his head. "And I don't mind her being complicated. Not one bit. Actually, it's part of what I love about her."

Eric's ears perked up. He'd always known that Dylan had a soft spot for Marina. Even when they were kids. But here he was saying the "L" word.

"I just wish she'd let me be a part of it all," Dylan continued. "The mood swings. The recovery. Her life. But she's convinced she's too far damaged for anybody to want to be around. She thinks she's a burden or some shit. So I'm stuck out here. With you fools. In the fucking friend zone."

Eric eyed Dylan's button up shirt, his dark hair combed back off his head. "That's an awful lot of hair gel for the friend zone, my brother."

Dylan bit back a smile and elbowed Eric in the ribs. "Shut the fuck up. I know it's not my usual look. And maybe I'm not *completely* in the friend zone. She takes me out of the bull pen every now and then."

"Right. Sexting. Well…" Eric raised one of the beers off the tray and waited until Dylan did the same.

"Here's to taking what we can get from women who are worth it."

Dylan's eyes flashed again. Half humor, half resignation.

"Here here."

* * *

Lexi lay in her bed just before dawn. She hadn't slept well. Maybe it had been all the junk food from the drive-in. Maybe it had been the excitement of seeing one of her favorite movies again.

She sighed. Who was she kidding?

It was because of all the residual energy from sitting side by side with Eric all night. They hadn't touched except for their shoulders. The way friends would casually touch. But she'd wanted so much more. She'd barely restrained herself from *taking* more.

Lexi turned her face into the pillow and groaned. She'd wanted to hold his hand. Wanted to tilt her head onto his shoulder or slide her feet into his lap. She'd wanted to do all sorts of couple stuff.

God. What was she doing?

Her mind flashed back to a few minutes after the boys had gone to concessions. Marina had just gotten back from the bathroom, something bright and cautious shining in her eyes as she'd climbed back into the truck.

"So, Lexi," she'd said, crossing her legs and facing her dead on. "About this whole casual hook up thing you've got going on with Eric…"

Lexi had been intrigued, although she was pretty sure they'd covered this subject less than an hour ago back at home. "Yeah?"

"Nothing could change your mind about that?"

"What do you mean?"

Marina had bit her lip, a little bit of her initial excitement failing and her nerves coming back. "Even if you knew something else? Maybe about what Eric wanted? It wouldn't change how you feel?"

Lexi had squinted her eyes. "What do you mean? Are you telling me you know something?"

Marina had taken a deep breath. She seemed to be weighing something in her mind. Unsure if she should speak up or not. She was just opening her mouth again when Eric and Dylan returned from the concessions, their hands piled up with junk food and beers. Lexi meant to press Marina further, but there were too many people around. Too many distractions.

Jake came back as well. Swiped a beer off the tray and kissed Eric full on the cheek. "Thanks for dinner, big boy," Jake had said and the laughter that overcame the group had driven the conversation from Lexi's mind.

Until now. What had Marina been about to say? Lexi was fairly certain that she was better off not knowing.

Needing to remind herself of her goals, Lexi flipped her feet out of bed and went over to the small desk next to her. She flipped open her laptop and opened the file. It was her latest screenplay. The one she was the proudest of. She picked a page at random and read a few lines. Instantly the characters warmed her. Centered her. Reminded her who she was. This was it. This was home. As a kid who'd never stayed in the same town longer than a month or two; this, her imagination, her goals, her skills, was the only home she'd ever known. That and her dad.

The sky was just starting to lighten at the edges and she knew she'd have to get up for work in a few hours anyways. An idea wormed its way into her head. Deciding not to think too hard on it, Lexi jumped in the shower. She dried off quickly and unceremoniously, tossed the towel back on the hook and slicked away the rest of the water droplets with her hands. She pulled on her jeans and her work T-shirt, yanked her hair back in a ponytail and called it a good job.

Her laptop under one hand, she patted Tulip's sleeping head on the way out of the house.

This was the right thing to do, Lexi told herself. She'd talked Eric's ear off about her dreams and goals. And now she needed to show him. She knew she couldn't completely trust herself not to fall for him. But maybe if she showed him what she was working with, then he'd double down on his own efforts to get her the hell out of here in August. She needed the reinforcements.

But that didn't keep her stomach from flipping as she drove the windy roads through the mountains to get to Eric's ranch. She hadn't been there since that first night.

Three, two, one. Bam. She came around that special curve that he'd shown her before. The one that revealed the entire valley in one fell swoop. It really was breathtakingly gorgeous. The kind of beauty that you didn't get used to. You just kept wanting to see over and over. The kind of beauty that somebody could build a life around.

That somebody like Eric could build a life around. Not her.

By the time she pulled up his driveway, the sky was a flirtatious pink, just starting to burn at the edge where the sun was waking up. And Eric was sitting on his front porch swing, cup of coffee in hand, just watching it. And grinning at her as she shoved out of her car.

"It's gone!" she called out to him, her eyes pinned to the place where the dilapidated barn had been just a few weeks ago.

"I'm a busy man, Lexi." He sipped his cup of coffee with a very proud, very self important look on his face.

"Well, not that I want to add to whatever is going on there," she motioned to the purposefully pompous expression. "But, yeah. Jeez, Eric. You really did it. It's like it was never even there."

He nodded. "Yup. Kind of sad in a way. But my architect just got the plans for the new barn approved. We're going to start rough construction next week. Then the next step will be the paddock."

She stood at the bottom of the porch steps squinting up at him. She was proud of him. No question. It took more than hard work to get this kind of thing going. It took vision. And drive. Even though she was worried about getting too stuck on him, in a way, he was the perfect person for her to have met this summer. He was living proof that knowing what you want and working hard for it paid off.

"You got any more of that?" she asked, nodding toward his cup of coffee.

"Kitchen."

She bounded up the steps and put the laptop in his lap. "Open it up, there's something on there I wanted to show you."

And then she disappeared into the house before she could watch him discover her manuscript. There was only so much a girl's heart could take.

Lexi wandered through his house and was surprised to see that a lot had changed. Seriously. Did this man ever sleep? He was at the hardware store a few hours everyday. He'd had a complete barn demo on his hands, and somehow he'd still managed to paint the living and dining room and get some furniture in there? Nice furniture too. The kind that made you want to sink right in and put your feet up.

Lexi approved of all the changes he was making to the farmhouse. Mismatched pillows on the couch. Family pictures on the walls. Cutting boards. Apples in a bowl. It was a nice house and she was happy he was really settling in.

Even if it did kind of make her stomach drop to see how well Montana fit Eric. And how easily she could see herself here, living with him. Staying with him.

Oh well. That's why she was only here for the summer.

She filled a cup of coffee and came back out onto the porch to the sound of Eric's laughter.

"What's so funny?"

He had the laptop open on his lap. "Scene two. The argument Sid is having with his mother."

Lexi flushed. She'd laughed out loud when she'd written that scene, but she hadn't known if anyone else would. She reached out and closed the laptop as she sat next to him on the swing. "Maybe you can read the rest later."

"Yeah," he took her cup of coffee from her. "Maybe you can scram so I can read the rest now."

She laughed and snatched the coffee back. But for the life of her couldn't think of anything else to say.

"It's really good so far, Lexi. Thank you for showing it to me."

She cleared her throat. "Well, I would have printed it. But I don't have a printer. And I would have emailed it, but I don't have your email. So, I just thought I'd bring the laptop." She was rambling. But what else was she supposed to do when she had this annoying bumper crop of butterflies in her stomach.

"It's exdavenport@gmail."

"Huh?" E. Davenport. Eric Davenport. Something about the combination of the first name and surname stuck in Lexi's mind.

"My email address. E for Eric. X for my middle name. And then my last name. Davenport."

"Davenport," she repeated, a little bit of snap on her tongue. "And X is your middle initial. Named for your father, no doubt."

Eric swung his eyes around to hers. Took a deceptively casual sip of his coffee. "Yes, actually. Xander. I always hated it. Always thought it sounded like a vampire's name or something."

Lexi didn't laugh. She was too busy getting tunnel vision on account of the rage-like feelings blaring through her. "Eric Xander Davenport."

She rose from the swing with such force that Eric had to steady it with one foot. "Eric fucking *Davenport*?"

He winced at her tone, but held her eyes in a steady gaze. He set his coffee aside and crossed his hands in front of him calmly. Like he was in a business meeting. "I take it you've heard of my family then?"

She let out a long, low breath. "Yeah, Eric. I've heard of Xander Davenport and Davenport Enterprises. I've heard of his son Eric. Golden child and heir to the throne. It's kind of hard not to hear about American royalty, Eric. Your company is only in the news every other fucking day. You're only billionaires."

This time he didn't wince. His expression hardened. "I didn't lie to you, Lexi."

No, he hadn't. But he hadn't been honest about who he was either. She stood and paced down to one end of the porch and back. The sun was really rising now and it cast a ruby halo around her. "You still should have told me."

* * *

At the anger, hurt, and yes, confusion on Lexi's face,

Eric's defensiveness eased. Not because he necessarily believed he should have told his most closely guarded secrets to just any woman he'd slept with twice, and worked and flirted with. But because Lexi was special. And that's why he should have told her.

"I don't advertise my wealth, Lexi," he tried to explain. "Especially where women are concerned."

She crossed her arms over her chest, looking like she was going to argue with him, then her shoulders loosened and she sighed. "You're right. I can only imagine the stuff people say to you. 'Mr. Davenport, can I buy you a drink, I'd like to talk to you about an investment opportunity.' 'Mr. Davenport, you're looking handsome tonight, can I offer myself on a silver platter for the low, low price of being your paid mistress?'"

Eric laughed at the disdainful and jealous expression that washed over her in that moment. "Something like that. But here it's more like, 'Eric, you need a ride tonight or will you meet us there?' 'Eric, come shoot some pool' 'Eric, you need a hand with that lumber delivery?'" He rose, and cupped her chin. "And then I meet this beautiful woman. Tough and nervous at the same time. And she came home with me. God only knows why. And all I wanted was to spend time with her. And she just waited for the rug to get pulled out. Any excuse to get the hell away from me. Even so, she treated me just like my closest friends. Like all the people who don't want anything more from me than my company. And I didn't have the heart to tell her the rest."

He took a step back from her and landed back on the porch swing. He snatched his coffee back up, took a huge swig and eyed her over the rim. "I'm sorry for deceiving you. It just felt so good to be liked for being me, and not for my money."

Lexi stared at him, then she came and sat down next to him. "Well, if you'd have *told* me, you'd have discovered that I would have liked you in spite of your money. Not because of it."

"It really doesn't change how you view me?"

"Of course it does!" She grabbed her coffee back up and took a huge slug of it. "You're a *billionaire*. If anything, it's just extremely uncommon, Eric. Randomly picking up a billionaire in a shitty bar in a one horse town is the equivalent of buying a ten cent goldfish at a pet store and finding out its a mermaid."

Eric threw his head back and laughed. Really laughed. "When you write the movie about us, make sure you include that line." He stroked a hand over her hair. "I get what you're saying though. It's just a lot of new information all at once." He sobered. "Just so you know, I'm not just throwing money at this ranch; it means something to me. It's a dream I've had in the back of my mind for a long time, ever since I'd come to visit my grandparents in the summers. I just didn't know how important it was to me until I came back."

Lexi nodded. "I understand dreams. I'm so proud you're going after yours."

He laid a hand over hers. "And I'm proud you're

pursuing yours. Because from what I've read, you have talent. Real talent, Lexi. And if you'll let me read the rest, if the rest of this manuscript is as good as the first few pages, I'd like to pass it along to some people I know. Would you accept that kind of help?"

She blinked. "Because you really think I'm good and not because I'm sleeping with you or you feel sorry for me? Then yes. I'll take that help."

"Good." He set his coffee aside and hooked one finger in the collar of her T-shirt. He pulled, revealing her slim, toned shoulder. A groan escaped him when he saw his own teeth marks there. "Now, I couldn't help but notice that this porch swing is, in fact, not a bed."

She giggled and shook her head. "A real master of observation we got here, people."

"Which, and correct me if I'm wrong, falls directly into the very strict set of rules you've set about where you and I can, you know, do the dirty."

Lexi raised an eyebrow at him, but she was smiling. And she kept smiling as he dragged her across his lap.

10

"Iris Hardware," Lexi answered the phone distractedly, one eye on the inventory sheet in front of her and one eye on the kid suspiciously lingering next to the magazine rack by the front door. That had been happening a lot since the Kardashians had started being on every single cover known to man. Didn't this kid have an internet connection? "Make a selection or scram," she called to the kid, holding the phone away from her voice. The kid jumped about a good foot in the air before scurrying out of the store.

"Sorry about that, how can I help you?" she spoke politely into the phone, crossing out a few things on the list in front of her.

"Yes, I'm looking for my son," a refined voice said on the other end of the line. "Eric Davenport? He doesn't seem to be answering his cell phone today."

Lexi froze. Great, just great. The first time she ever interacts with Eric's mom is when she's yelling at a thirteen-year-old perv for getting his jollies in the front of the store. Grand. Exactly the way you want to be introduced to your boyfriend's billionaire mother.

Lexi winced yet again. God. How many times was she going to do that? Refer to Eric as her boyfriend in her head? They were so *not* that. And in the week since the drive-in movie, she'd made double sure of it. She'd kept such a tight lid on her feelings, Eric had pretty much stopped flirting with her in person.

Text or phone calls were still fair play, however.

Anyone but the most careful observer would believe they were just friends. If that. Maybe even just work colleagues.

But try as she might, she was having trouble convincing herself of the same thing. The word 'boyfriend' was popping up in her head every twenty seconds. Stupid, traitorous brain. It was starting to be annoying.

"Hello? Hello? Is anyone there?" The voice came through the line and Lexi jumped.

Perfect. Just perfect. And now she was spacing out on the line. She could only imagine what Eric's mom thought of her right now.

"Right. Hi. Yes, sorry. I'm here. You're looking for Eric?"

"Yes, dear."

"He's out back with a delivery. I'll run out and get him."

"Hold on one second, dear. Is this Lexi?"

Lexi cleared her throat. "Yes, ma'am."

"Well, it's lovely to meet you over the phone. I've heard quite a bit about you."

Lexi had no idea what to say. She had the insane urge to put on an English accent. Instead she fell back on old habits and melted a little further into her drawl. "Is that right?"

"Yes, my son says you're an extremely gifted screenwriter."

Her stomach flipped. He'd said that? She knew he'd been impressed by the manuscript she'd shown him a few weeks ago, but she hadn't figured on him talking to his mom about it. She scrambled for something more to say.

"I try."

"Now, honey, I'm wondering if you can help me out with something?"

"Yes, ma'am."

"My son seems to be rather taken with you. Which has been like music to my ears considering how hard this past year has been on him."

Lexi's hand tightened on the phone and she made a small noise to show she was still listening, but it was about the best she could do.

"It's very important to me that he make it back to L.A. this weekend for a fundraising gala we're attending. However, Eric won't commit. It's understandable, given his ex Brianne will be there with... Well, Brianne is actually the event planner. But the man throwing the party, Gio Esposito, is a colleague and friend of the family, and while there is no shortage of fundraisers in our business, there are plenty of people who know why Eric left L.A., and I think it's high time he shows them he's not running anymore. Which can only truly happen if he returns to L.A. and what better way to return than at a party in which Brianne and Gabe are in attendance? I'm wondering if you can help push Eric in the right direction by agreeing to attend the gala with him. What do you say?"

Lexi blinked. "I—" That was as far as Lexi could get before her brain just up and shorted out. "Um, I don't think—" she began, but that was all she could say before Eric came in from the back, wiping his forehead with the handkerchief he kept in the back pocket of his jeans.

"It's hotter than hell out there," he said, lifting off his sweaty baseball cap and tossing it on the cashier counter. "We got anything to drink around here?"

"Oh, Mrs. Davenport, Eric just walked in. I'll hand you over now." Without wasting another second Lexi dropped the phone into Eric's hand like it was made of hot coals.

Eric's eyes went wide with surprise and he raised the receiver to his ear. "Mom?"

He listened for a few seconds before his expression fell into one of resigned exasperation. "Yeah. Uh huh. Uh huh." He turned and looked at Lexi full in the face and she found herself inexplicably blushing. "Well, I wouldn't exactly describe her that way myself, but yes, she's really great. One of the good ones."

Lexi turned away from the laser focus in Eric's blue

eyes. She'd never had a man discuss her with his mother right in front of her before. Especially when that mother had just invited her into said man's life in a way that completely broke every rule that Lexi herself had set out for them.

"Well, she's got a life of her own, so I don't know. Right. You got it. Uh huh. Oh for fuck's sake, Mom. Beat me to death with it, why don't you!"

Lexi turned back in complete shock. She surveyed him with her mouth wide open. Did he really just say the f-word to his own mother? To the sweet, sophisticated aristocrat that Lexi had just finished talking to?

But Eric was grinning into the phone affectionately. "You win. You win. Yes, ma'am. Alright. Love you too."

Eric hung up the phone and dropped his forehead into his hand and rubbed at his temples before he snatched up his hat and jammed it back on his head. He crossed to the other side of the counter where Lexi was resolutely sorting packets of seeds into a revolving stand.

"So…" He leaned back against the counter, one ankle crossed over the other, the ball cap low over his eyes. His T-shirt was sweaty at the neck. He'd never looked less like a billionaire and more like a cowboy. "My mom says you're 'sweet as pie.'"

Lexi snorted and raised an eyebrow. "Is that when you told her that's not the way you'd describe me?"

He grinned and nodded before a different look fell over his face. One she couldn't even begin to interpret. "You want to go to L.A. this weekend?"

"Wow." Lexi kept sorting seed packets. "I'm not exactly sure what to say to that."

"Maybe we should start with what my mother told you on the phone and I'll correct the fabrications as we go along."

"Fabrications?" Lexi raised her eyebrows.

"My mother has been known to stretch truths to serve her own reality."

Lexi smiled tightly. "Ah. Well. She invited me to come to some sort of fundraising gala this weekend. With you. There's going to be some big-wig businessman slash family friend there. Someone named Gio? Cool name."

"It is a cool name. And Gio's a cool guy. I'd actually enjoy seeing him. I'd enjoy seeing quite a few people."

"So part of you wants to go?"

He hesitated, then shrugged. "Yes."

"But part of you doesn't want to?"

When he cocked a brow, Lexi sighed. "Your mom mentioned that Brianne and Gabe would be there, as a couple I presume..." She zipped her eyes up to his. "It's totally understandable why you wouldn't want to see them, Eric."

Eric groaned and dropped his head back, scrubbed his hands over his eyes. "Understandable, sure, but total bullshit."

"What?"

"I don't give a fuck about seeing them together, Lexi."

"Are you kidding?"

"No, I'm not kidding. It really doesn't bother me anymore. Sure, it doesn't feel *good* to think about how much time we wasted, Brianne and I. Or the fact that when I started dating Brianne, I knew Gabe was into her and ignored that. I could have saved us all a lot of heartache if I'd been a better friend to both of them. But they're together now. So much happier than they were when I was between them. And I'm glad. I really am. Even more than that, I'm happy here. Happier than I've ever been. So…"

Even though it broke every single one of her self-preservation rules, even though it was broad daylight and public and their place of work, Lexi couldn't help herself. She reached forward, took him by the collar of his shirt and kissed him. Hard. It was more of a brand than a sensual moment. And when she finally released him and went back to sorting seeds, she could feel the echo of the kiss on her lips.

"What was that for?" He had one hand to his mouth like he was feeling the same echo she was.

She shrugged. "You're a good man."

He let out a long string of air. "So you want to go with this good man to L.A. this weekend?"

Not answering his direct question, she turned to him and crossed her arms over her chest. "If it wasn't about Brianne and Gabe, then why were you hesitating going in the first place?"

Eric hesitated. "I'm not sure you'll like the answer."

"Try me."

He stared her dead in the eye. "We're already halfway

through the summer. I didn't want to waste a whole weekend away from you."

Lexi's stomach pulled tight. It was like nerves and elation both had one end of the tug of war rope inside her. "Oh."

His eyes raced over her face then he shrugged. "Plus, I told you I'm happy here. Montana feels more like home to me than L.A. ever did. So if I'm going to spend a weekend away from my ranch, my friends, you, well… L.A. wouldn't be my first choice."

Jesus. She had to step carefully here.

On one hand, traveling together, to see his family and friends no less, was the most couple-ish thing two people could do. On the other hand, she'd be going to L.A., where she'd soon be living anyway. She could get an unexpected preview into what her exciting new life would look like.

"Would we maybe have time to check out places where I could live in August?"

"Of course. The gala is only for a few hours on Saturday night. So we could close the store early Friday and fly back late on Sunday. Take the weekend in between to help you get to know the city a little bit."

God that sounded good. Eric knew L.A. It would be really nice to be introduced to it by somebody she could trust.

She bit her lip. "People would assume I'm your girlfriend, wouldn't they?"

"It's inevitable that some people would assume it. But we can introduce you however you want. My friend, colleague, or kick ass screenwriter who I think is brilliant."

Lexi flushed and turned away. She did some quick calculations. Just as the trip would be an unexpected treat, it would also be an unexpected expense. The airline ticket would probably drain half the money in her bank account. Then there would be the expense of the hotel…

"Look, it sounds cool. And I don't want to make you go alone. But I should save the money for when I move."

Eric opened his mouth and Lexi instantly raised a threatening finger.

Her eyes narrowed into slits. "Don't you dare offer to pay for my plane ticket."

Eric raised his hands in surrender. "I would never do such a horrible thing." He cleared his throat. "But, um, as I was going to fly myself down there, I just thought you wouldn't mind riding in my plane with me."

Lexi's mind went blank. "*Your* plane?"

"I'm a registered pilot. I keep a plane over at the airport in Bozeman."

"You're a pilot. Of your own plane."

He rubbed the back of his neck. "It's no big deal. You'd like it, I swear. It's fun."

"And me coming along wouldn't be an added expense for you? You know, extra fuel because the plane will weigh more?"

"I assure you, you coming along would not increase my flight expenses. And I'd really love your company, Lexi. So what do you say?"

What *could* she say? She wanted to go with him. So

she took a deep breath and braced herself to jump. "Well, I guess I better find myself a fancy dress, huh?"

* * *

Two hours later, Eric let her leave work early in order to get ready for the trip. As soon as she walked through the front door, she took a moment to scratch a wagging Tulip on the chin and called to Marina. When she heard something in the kitchen she headed that way.

"Marina! Can I try on that fancy dress you have and maybe borrow it for the—"

Lexi came up short. Marina was up on the kitchen counter, a spilled vase of flowers behind her, and her legs wrapped around Dylan's waist. His hand was up her blouse and his mouth latched onto her throat.

As soon as he realized they had company, Dylan straightened Marina's clothes and quickly turned around, blocking her from Lexi's view to give Marina a second to compose herself.

Lexi's eyes couldn't help but scan up and down Dylan. He was a very attractive man currently sporting a humongous bulge in his pants. She tucked her tongue in her cheek.

"Whatcha doin?" she asked innocently.

"Oh god," Marina groaned, hopping down from the counter and stepping around Dylan. "I'm sorry you had to see that."

"I'm not." Lexi leaned against the door jamb and

patted Tulip as he sauntered past. "That was hot as hell."

Marina blushed furiously and Dylan let out a low chuckle. "I knew I liked you."

Lexi grinned. "Sorry to interrupt something that looked extremely beneficial for all parties involved."

Marina blushed and pulled her hair back into a ponytail. "You, uh, said you needed to borrow something of mine?"

"Yeah. If it fits, and if it's alright with you, I wanted to borrow that dress of yours this weekend."

"What dress?"

"You know that fancy black one that you bought for your friend's art show?"

Marina's eyes whipped to Dylan and back to Lexi. She went beet red. "Oh, right."

Dylan frowned, then crossed his arms over his chest.

"Art show?" Dylan asked. "What friend had an art show?"

"Oh, um, no one. It was nothing. Maybe we could talk about it later." Marina seriously looked as if she was about to catch on fire from embarrassment.

She darted away, and Dylan seemed about to go after her. To Lexi's surprise, Tulip darted around him and sat on his haunches, planting himself in between Marina and Dylan and Lexi. He didn't look unfriendly, but the dog was definitely sending a message.

Dylan looked down at the dog and stepped back. "Good boy," he murmured.

And if Lexi had ever had a single reservation about

Dylan pursuing Marina, it completely evaporated in that second. He was praising Tulip for protecting Marina, even if it was from himself. That was a good man. That was a really good man.

Marina returned a second later holding the black silk dress. She handed it right to Lexi but Dylan intercepted it, rubbed the silk between his fingers and held it up in the air for a better look.

"This is a really nice dress, Mari." His eyes bored into hers. If Lexi hadn't been quite so curious as to what was going to happen next, she might have given them a little more privacy.

"You bought this for the opening of my furniture show in Portland, didn't you?"

Lexi knew from Eric that Dylan designed and made furniture. He made a lot of utilitarian furniture for people around here. But he also made some of the loveliest pieces she'd ever seen that he shipped off to be sold in galleries in the bigger cities.

Marina, still looking at the ground, nodded her head.

"But you didn't come," Dylan said, his voice low and insistent. "I waited for you that night. But you never showed."

Lexi gently tugged the dress out of Dylan's hand and stepped back. She didn't need to be here for this. It was too invasive. But she froze when she saw tears shining in Marina's eyes. She couldn't leave while her friend was crying.

"I was there, Dylan. I went inside for a minute. But I

hid. I hid behind that big staircase in the middle of that room. And then I left."

"Why did you leave?"

Lexi started inching away again, not wanting to break the spell between them by making any abrupt movements.

"Because I knew that if we saw each other, all dressed up like that, in the middle of that fancy room, with the champagne and so far from home. I knew that everything would have changed between us."

Dylan stepped closer to Marina, wrapped his hand around the back of her neck. "You were right," he growled and kissed her. Marina whimpered, threw her arms around Dylan, and wholeheartedly returned the kiss.

Lexi finally left the kitchen and headed into her room, where she let out a big gasp of air.

Wow.

Would they be together now? Would they finally be able to get out of their own way and just make it work? Somehow, Lexi wasn't quite so sure. She knew all about being in your own way.

She laid the dress across her bed. So simple, so beautiful. Such a perfect illusion. She knew, as she looked at it, that while she was wearing it, she'd feel like a different person. But the minute she took it off, she'd go back to being plain old Lexi Fischer. Broke. Determined. Tough. Loner.

She sat next to the dress on her bed and stroked one hand over it. She repeated that last word out loud. Just in case she'd been fool enough to ignore it the first time.

"Loner."

11

Eric hadn't thought there was much that could surprise him anymore. He'd been to almost every country in the world. Tasted thousands of the most expensive foods. Played poker at tables with five figure buy-ins. He'd climbed mountains, scuba dived, jumped out of planes, and even swum with sharks.

But nothing, absolutely nothing, prepared him for the experience of flying with Lexi. She'd told him she'd never been in a plane before, but seeing her now, hands clasped to her chest as if she were praying, staring out the window as they kissed the outer edge of a cumulous cloud, tears in her gorgeous dark eyes…

He hadn't been prepared for how it would feel to give her something like this.

He hadn't been prepared for the realization that slammed into him in that moment. He loved her.

Despite the fact they were so different. Despite the fact they'd only known each other for a few weeks.

Despite the fact she was so damn determined to leave him behind in August to pursue her dreams in L.A.

He loved her.

And he wanted her to know it.

I love you. The words strained at the edge of his tongue like pit bulls at the end of their leashes. He'd never wanted to say it so badly in his life. But he knew how it would make her feel. He knew how it would put a pin in her balloon. And more than anything in his life, he didn't want to deflate her right now. Not when she was looking at him like he'd hung the fucking moon.

So he swallowed the words down.

She squeaked as the sun caught the right angle over a river in the distance and it lit up like a snake on fire. Her pointing finger was the only thing that indicated to him what she was seeing.

"Lexi, baby, you gotta speak," he said as he grinned at her. "I don't know what you mean unless you speak."

She took a deep breath. "It's. Just. Like. Aladdin."

Eric burst out laughing. Of all the things she could have said, he never would have guessed that would be it. "I can show you the world…" He sang loudly and off key and had Lexi both laughing and grimacing.

"Except in our version, you're an actual prince and I'm the raggedy beggar." She smiled as she said the words but they dropped the bottom out of Eric's stomach.

"Lex, you don't actually think that do you?"

She blinked, then shook her head. "No, not the way it sounded," she responded. "I just meant that if there ever was an example of how our lives are different, this is it." She gestured around at the mountains in the distance, the ice cream scoops of cumulous clouds all around them.

"Yeah, but we're both here in this plane. This is *our* life right now."

He regretted his words the second that Lexi narrowed her eyes at him, a hint away from suspicious. "I guess," she acquiesced. "For the summer anyways."

"Sure." The word felt like gravel in his mouth, but he was the one making this harder on himself. Why was he pushing her? She'd made the rules very clear. All he had to do was follow them. And here he was trying to change things around. It wasn't fair to either of them.

A few hours later, they landed the plane at the airport and Eric took a deep breath as he grabbed their bags out of the back. He was suddenly deeply regretting having done this.

He wanted to give Lexi the world. Take her on a hundred plane rides if it meant her reacting the way she had. But they were about to get into a chauffeured car that would lead them to the glitziest hotel in town. Along the way there would be a hundred indicators of his money. Of his life before he'd moved to Montana. In trying to give her a special introduction to L.A., he would only be emphasizing the differences between them. Why the hell had he thought this was a good idea?

Because he hadn't wanted to spend even a weekend away from her.

Lexi took her bag from him and tossed it over her

back. "Something wrong?"

"No," he said quickly. "No, I'm just hungry."

"Yeah, I could use some dinner."

"Well, I know just the place."

He led her to his private car in the distance. Deciding to throw caution, and the rules, to the wind, he reached back and took her by the hand.

Either she was too distracted or she was grateful for the comfort. Lexi didn't pull her hand back the way he'd half expected her to do.

She stopped short beside him, however, when he pulled open the back door of a sleek, black Rolls Royce.

"My lady," he said, halfway bowing down to her.

She gave a surprised, confused little laugh and slid into the seat.

"Eric!"

Eric turned and was instantly enveloped in the arms of George, his driver. He hadn't seen him in months. "George!"

The two men hugged and came away grinning at one another. Lexi scrambled out of the seat and came to stand next to the two men.

"George, this is Lexi. My good friend and date to the gala tomorrow."

Lexi held out her hand to George, her eyes racing all over him as she took in his uniform.

"Nice to meet you, pretty lady," George said, taking her hand and pressing a kiss to the back of it. Lexi's eyes grew wide.

He clapped George on the shoulder. "We're headed to the Beverly Wilshire."

"Ahh," George said. "Nice digs."

"For the lady," Eric corrected, before either George or Lexi could get the wrong idea. "I'll be at my house."

George's eyes clouded just a bit in confusion, but he nodded his head and jogged around to the driver's side of the car, remembering that Eric preferred to get his own car door.

Eric and Lexi slid into the car and George pulled smoothly away from the curb.

"Do you make him dress like that?" Lexi whispered to Eric and George's laughter exploded through the car.

Eric bit the inside of his cheek to keep from laughing as well and pressed the button that put the glass up between them and George.

"It's a very standard driver's uniform. Although George admittedly chooses jauntier hats than most."

"Ah," Lexi said, looking out her window and chewing at one of her fingernails. It was a nervous tic that Eric had never seen her do before. Without thinking too hard on it, he reached up and took her hand. She looked down at their laced fingers and then back out the window. The palm trees whizzed past.

"Isn't the Beverly Wilshire a really fancy hotel?" Her voice was quiet.

Eric wasn't quite sure how to answer that, since he was fairly certain she'd view it as charity. "You'll be very comfortable there."

She turned to him, a little of that skeptical spark back in her eyes. "Why aren't I just staying at your house? Isn't it big enough?"

"Yeah, it is. I just thought you'd be more comfortable if it didn't appear we were going home together."

"Oh. Right." Her fingers snaked away from his and her thumbnail went right back in her mouth.

Eric would have paid a ridiculously large sum of money to know what she was thinking right now. But she kept her face averted.

They cruised through the city and into Venice Beach until Eric knocked on the glass at George. "Pull over for just a sec!"

Eric jumped out at the curb, tugging Lexi along with him.

He grinned back at her as she frowned in confusion, looking back at their car idling at the curb.

Eric pulled her through an unmarked door, sandwiched between a trashy nail salon and a little grocery. They stepped into a little restaurant. Well, sort of a restaurant. It was dingy, with a few scattered tables with folding chairs and newspapers spread out over them as makeshift tablecloths. A few patrons in the corner were eating something out of one big bowl while they played cards. They barely looked up when Eric and Lexi came through.

Eric didn't pause, he walked right through another door, a swinging one, and into the kitchen.

"Eric!" A huge man came barreling around from

behind a huge stove. Something bubbled there that smelled like delicious sin.

"Rico!" Eric allowed himself to be hugged and kissed on either cheek by his old friend.

"And who is this little slice of nice?" Rico asked, raising his eyebrows at Lexi.

She couldn't help but laugh as she allowed herself to be hugged by Rico as well. "I'm Lexi. Eric's... lady friend."

Rico's eyebrows raised even further. "Nah, darlin'. Eric's your man friend. Not the other way around. Don't you forget it."

Lexi laughed again. Harder this time and Eric could have kissed Rico for loosening her up. But his stomach growled and reminded him why they were there.

"What's good tonight?" he asked, sniffing at the air. He turned to Lexi. "Rico makes one thing every day and it's the only thing he'll serve. Whatever catch is the freshest."

"Tonight it's shrimp jambalaya over rice."

Lexi raised her eyes. "Jambalaya?" she asked in surprise.

"Yes, baby," Rico answered. "I'm born and raised in Louisiana. Nobody makes it like I do."

"He's right," Eric assured her.

"Smells good enough," Lexi said, shrugging.

Rico laughed as he dished them portions. "I like her. She's not slobbering all over everything trying to impress you, son."

Eric bit the inside of his cheek. "I think it literally goes against her DNA to try and impress me."

Lexi turned and looked at him in surprise.

"Yeah," Eric continued. "It's been me trying to do all the impressing since day one."

"Well, that's the natural order of things, then," Rico said, handing them the food in plastic Tupperware.

"We need one more portion. For George." Eric looked around and reached into the cooler in the corner. "And add three cokes to the tab."

"What tab?" Rico asked, frowning at Eric and handing over the food to Lexi. "You know your money's no good here, son."

"You know he's a billionaire, right?" Lexi asked, sounding as unimpressed with it as Eric knew she was. "He can afford this."

Rico laughed again. "Yeah, but he's a billionaire with heart. He knows what he did. Now pop two of those cokes open, for the non drivers, and I'll give you a splash of something that'll make your night extra special."

Lexi did as he said and then grinned when he pulled a flask out of his pocket and dumped something into the cokes.

He shooed them out of the kitchen, hugging Eric goodbye and kissing Lexi on the cheek.

"Tell her what you did for me, son," Rico called out as Eric and Lexi made their way out of the restaurant. Eric just waved and shook his head.

They slid back into the car and Eric handed George's

food up front. "Let's find someplace with a view to eat this dinner, Georgie."

Half an hour later, the three of them were sitting on the boardwalk, eating their dinners out of Tupperware and people watching.

"So, what'd you do for Rico?" Lexi asked, her mouth full of food.

"Ah. We don't have to talk about it," Eric said, shifting uncomfortably.

"He paid off a bunch of debts that Rico owed when he owned this big restaurant over on the other side of L.A."

Eric glared at George, who paid him no mind.

"He'd got himself into trouble with the wrong people. Eric got him away with his knee caps still intact. And Rico set up over there. Where we just were. A much smaller operation."

"Hmm," Lexi hummed around her food, her eyes watching all that was Venice Beach. Person after person walking by. Rollerbladers. Dogs in purses. Jugglers. Even at this time of night it was still bumping with activity.

Again, Eric would have paid a fortune to know what she was thinking. And again, she said nothing to let him in on the secret.

They just drank their spiked cokes and ate their food and went on their way. She leaned her head back on the headrest behind her and let her eyes flutter closed for a second. And when they pulled up at the Wilshire, she was even more silent than before.

They got out, with George promising to see Lexi

tomorrow when he gave her a ride to the gala. Eric asked him for a little time so that he could get her settled in her room.

She was silent as they walked through the grand lobby. Silent as he checked her in. Silent in the elevator, with its elevator man who Eric tipped. Silent as he walked her down the plush, opulent hallway.

God, he inwardly groaned. Why hadn't he thought to put her up someplace a little bit… less? If she was reeling from seeing the hallway, then she was in no way prepared to see her room.

He had to grind his teeth as he swung open her door and she walked into the humongous suite. Bigger than Marina's whole house.

He set her bag down on the chaise lounge in front of the floor-to-ceiling windows. He took a deep breath and turned to face the music.

She stood there, one hand over her mouth, with a look on her face like he'd just dragged her into a slum. There was awe. And, he was surprised to see, fear.

"I can't stay here alone," she finally sputtered.

"Why?"

"I'll ruin something. Or make a mess. Or they won't believe that I'm a guest and they'll kick me out."

"Of course that won't happen." He stepped toward her but she took a step back like a wild animal. "Lexi, none of those things are going to happen."

"Will you stay?" she asked him, her eyes as big and wide and round as a child's.

If he hadn't been in love with her before, it would have been a done deal now. There was no chance he would ever deny this woman anything. Ever.

"I'd love to. I just wasn't sure you'd want me to."

She turned to him, her arms clasped in front of her. "I want you to."

"Then absolutely. Let me run down and get my bag from George. Here." He shifted her toward the little breakfast table with an arrangement of flowers on it and strode over to the mini bar. He pulled out a little shooter of whiskey, a glass, and some ice cubes. "Drink that. It'll take the edge off. I swear."

She looked up at him and nodded. He couldn't stand it. Going down on his knees in front of her he pushed her hair back over her shoulder. "I'll be right back."

When he returned she was sitting exactly where he'd left her and her glass was empty of whiskey. He tossed his bag on the floor, ripped one hand through his hair, got a whiskey for himself and sat down next to her at the breakfast table.

"Alright," he said, staring her right in the eye. "I knew better than to expect you to jump up and down on the bed, or pop champagne, but you're acting like I brought you to a murder scene. It's just a hotel room for god sakes!" Lexi reached over, took a little sip of his whiskey and took a deep breath. "I know, I know. And I'm being ungrateful."

"Lex, baby, you're not. I just want to know if you're alright in there. Blink if you can hear me."

Lexi smiled a little and shimmied out of her light coat she'd worn on the plane. He could see that her T-shirt was a little sweaty around the neck and Eric wondered why she'd kept it on if she'd been hot.

"It's just...I've never been on a plane before. Never been in a chauffeured car. Never had jambalaya." She dropped her eyes. "Never seen the ocean before."

He tried as hard as he could not to drop his jaw. "Never been to the beach before and I take you to the Venice fucking boardwalk? I should be shot."

She ignored him. "I've never stayed in a hotel before. Motels, yes. Hotel? Never. And certainly not one that is fit for the president."

Eric looked around them and winced. "It is a little much, I guess."

"It's beautiful. I'm just overwhelmed. And it feels weird, too, knowing I'll be back here in August and never see stuff like this again. It makes me want to soak it all in, you know? But more than that..." She took a deep breath. "I want to soak in all this time with *you*."

Eric's stomach twisted and he realized that this was it. This was a moment he might not be able to make it back from. He was going to cross a line with her. He just hoped it wasn't a deal breaker.

"Lex, you know I'm not going to actually leave you in August, right?"

She sat up straight, her eyes going from blurry and overwhelmed to laser bright. "What?"

"I mean, will I give you space? Absolutely. Will we

be together? Sounds like that's a no. But will I just up and lose your number? Hell no. Lex, I'm here. In your life. And I'm not going to drag you back to Montana, where you obviously don't want to be. But I'm sure as hell not abandoning you. And when I come back to L.A. to see my parents or whatever, you know who I'm going to call? You. Every time. If you're trying to really hack it on your own, then, yeah, it'll take a while to see this kind of cream. If that's what you want. But anytime you want a fancy dinner, nice champagne, a night on the town, a night in a hotel like this, you call me, Lex. And then you get it. I promise."

Her mouth opened up and then closed. Her eyes were too bright, too focused. She rose and then sat. And then rose again. He waited for her to say something. Anything. But when no words came, he reached out for her. But she took a step back.

"I need a second."

She took another step back. And another. And then she was in the bathroom. It was only a few seconds before Eric heard the shower running.

Wow. Good one, Davenport. He'd known the risks when he'd talked to her like that. And now he'd driven her away. He just hoped he hadn't driven her away for good.

12

Lexi took one deep breath after another, thinking of all the movies set in L.A. that she's seen.

Beverly Hills Cop, Pretty Woman, 9 to 5, Terminator, Dirty Rotten Scoundrels, Sunset Boulevard, Singing in the Rain.

They should have prepared her for what the city was like, but now that she'd seen it, she was scared. Everything reminded her that she was small and insignificant and suddenly Lexi was completely convinced that if she moved to L.A. she was going to fail.

Fail at her dream.

Fail at life.

What was she going to do?

Hurriedly, she stripped and stepped into the shower, hoping the water would help her regain her composure. Sure enough, as she scraped shampoo through her hair and soap over her body, her rational mind started to take over.

This was normal, she told herself. Normal to be scared

when staring something as big as L.A. in the face. It was especially hard given she was with Eric, learning how different they were. Accepting that she wouldn't be able to rely on him when she was on her own.

But was that even true?

With a deep sigh, Lex turned the water off and dried off. Then she scraped condensation off the bathroom mirror and stared at her reflection.

She was the same old Lexi. In this life she had her father and herself. The two people she could always count on.

And Eric, a stubborn voice inside her head reminded her. Don't forget you have Eric.

That's what he'd been telling her. That he was always going to be there for her, no matter what happened in August.

Eric who was sitting outside that door. Eric who'd respected every boundary she'd put up. Eric who'd brought her here to show her the first step in getting her dream. Eric who'd promised not to get her stuck in Montana. Eric who wasn't going to abandon her in August.

Eric who made her feel safe. And powerful. And believed in the power of her dreams even when she didn't.

Before she knew what she was doing, Lexi flung open the bathroom door, steam billowing out around her.

Eric looked up instantly from where he still sat at the breakfast table. His shirt was partially unbuttoned, his shoes in a pile on the floor. The dim, ambient lamplight outlined his perfect, movie star face. God. She was such a goner.

Lexi pushed that thought aside and strode toward him. Like a magnet to metal. He was calling to her. In this overwhelming city, he was her safe place. A beacon of all things good and calm.

Eric's eyes dipped from her toes all the way back up as he took her in. Naked as sin, golden and pink and dewy from the shower. He could have sat where he was, waited for her to come all the way to him. But he didn't. He met her halfway across the floor, knowing exactly what she was coming to him for.

They tumbled together onto the big sectional couch that separated the bedroom of the hotel suite from the living area. Lexi gasped as she felt the plush material come up against her back.

Eric was over her, surrounding her. Everywhere.

He reared back from her and tore off his clothes with the speed of a man possessed. He needed her as badly as she needed him. There was something burning in his eyes; whether it was the same thing she was feeling, Lexi had no idea, but it was setting them both on fire.

He was naked against her now, gripping her tightly, like he was terrified she would disappear if he let go.

Lexi, riding on the back of that same fear, clamped her teeth into his shoulder the way he'd often done to her. Eric groaned into her skin as she held him in place in every way possible.

He reared back from her and spread her legs wide. He

was looking down at her like she was a feast and he was a starving man. Lexi needed him, her body burned for him. But she could either lay there and be devoured, or she could do some devouring herself. Before he could go down on her, Lexi slid herself further down on the couch, so he was straddling her shoulders.

Eric's eyes flamed bright and hard. "Lex," he growled out in warning.

But it was a warning she didn't heed. Leaning up, she fisted the base of his cock and ran her tongue, just once, in a perfect, firm circle around the head.

His entire body went stiff as a board and Lexi was thrilled to see that his hand gripped the back of the couch so hard his knuckles had gone white. So she did it again.

This time he gasped out, as if he were in physical pain.

Looking up at him, keeping eye contact, Lexi licked her palm so that she could jack him more easily. Then she took him into her mouth swallowing him down as far as she could and following each movement of her mouth with her hand so that he was under a constant onslaught of feeling. He was big, so big that she couldn't even come close to taking him all the way. But she did the best she could, swirling her tongue and swallowing hard.

"Jesus, Lex. I'm going to— Damn, girl, I'm going to—"

And she wanted him to. She wanted to swallow all of him down. Taste him in that primal way. But then his hand was tangling in her hair and he was pulling her off.

"I want it. I want it," she panted, staring up at him.

"You're going to get it," he promised as he swiveled around, so he still straddled her shoulders, but facing away from her now.

He put a big palm on either of her thighs and spread her. There were no pleasantries. He simply leaned down and absolutely consumed her.

Lexi had never been more turned on or closer to coming. She wasn't sure she'd be able to hold on much longer. So as soon as she felt the first echoes of her orgasm start to tear through her, she reared up, took Eric by the hips and guided his cock back into her mouth.

Maybe it was the fact that she was about to come, maybe it was the change in position. But this time Lexi was able to swallow him almost all the way down. He slammed into the back of her throat and she swallowed and swallowed around him, breathing through her nose.

Eric went even more wild and Lexi's hips went taut, lifting up from the couch and into his face. Her orgasm electrified her, whipping through her so hard she could feel it everywhere. In every molecule of her soul.

And then Eric was coming too. Pumping into her mouth and splashing down her throat. She relished it, swallowing everything he gave her until he rolled to the side, both of their bodies trembling with the aftershocks.

"Holy shit," he mumbled before he twisted around and pulled her toward him. "I think we both really needed that."

Lexi couldn't help but smile as he nuzzled into her

damp hair, traced a hand over her belly, then gripped her hips and pulled her into him so he was spooning her.

Never in all their time together had they snuggled like this. Lexi had believed that they never would.

But with the city racing below them and their futures racing out in front of them, it didn't feel wrong to lay there with him. To feel his strong, steady heartbeat against her back and his arm banded across her body. It didn't feel wrong, even when he grabbed a blanket off the back of the couch and draped it over them.

"This doesn't count, by the way," he murmured into her hair right before sleep took them both.

"What?" she asked blearily.

"This doesn't count as breaking a rule." He smoothed a sleepy hand over her hair and tugged her just a little bit closer. She relished the heat kicking off his skin. "Technically, we never made it to the bed."

Whether she'd admit it in the morning or not she wasn't sure. But Lexi fell asleep with a smile on her face that night.

* * *

At noon the next day, Eric and Lexi were at the third place on Lexi's list of potential places to live once she moved to L.A. Like the two places before it, it was a dump, and as she pulled Eric around the corner of the small house, he was sure she was going to burst into panicked tears. He was prepared to comfort her, to tell her that together they'd find a place that was perfect for her and that yes, damn it, that meant she would accept his help. To his surprise, however, Lexi flung herself into Eric's arms even as she hopped up and down in excitement.

"I would get my own bathroom here!" She pulled away from him and stared him dead in the eye, just in case he didn't realize what a big, flipping deal that was. "MY. OWN. BATHROOM. In the history of time that has never happened for me."

Eric swallowed hard. He was about to point out the place was a dump. Instead he blurted out the biggest thing the place had going against it. "But your roommate would be... a dude."

"Even at Marina's we still have to share. Timing showers and such. And even though it's kind of a small bathroom and the shower was a little dingy WHO CARES right? Because... Wait, what?"

Feeling like an ass at the confused look on her face, Eric swiped a hand through his hair, thought about muttering nothing, then sighed. "It's just, when you said your roommate would be someone named Aubrey, I assumed it would be a woman."

Lexi's brows furrowed. "Aubrey can be a name for either gender."

"Right. Right. It's just... I'm pretty sure he was straight too."

"Your point?"

He sighed again. Told himself he was an idiot for being jealous of the youthful, muscular Aubrey—that wasn't what he and Lexi were about, he reminded himself—then shook his head. Quicksand. Don't be her quicksand. "Nothing," he said. "No point. If you like the place and you like Aubrey, I'm happy for you."

Lexi tilted her head to the side. Stared at him. And when her eyes widened, he could tell she'd realized what he was feeling. He waited for her to gently admonish him. Instead, she slid

her hands up his chest and back around his neck.

"I didn't notice if Aubrey was a straight man or a female lion. I was too busy losing my mind over having my own bathroom." And with that, she brought her grinning mouth to his.

* * *

To hell with the rules, Lexi thought to herself, even as she kissed Eric. He'd looked so damn cute, his hair all tousled from yanking at it, his expression disgruntled. No, not disgruntled—jealous, she'd finally realized. Jealous of a stranger named Aubrey. As if any man could hold a candle to Eric and what he made Lexi feel.

Still, his jealousy pleased her. It made her feel cherished. And for once, she didn't think about quicksand or whether she and Eric were doing the right thing by spending time together. Instead, she simply did what she wanted to, and that was to touch him. Kiss him.

They were still kissing on the street corner when a group of kids on bikes hooted and hollered as they rode past. Even then, Eric just held her tighter and it was a full thirty seconds before he released her and pulled away, his eyes cloudy and his hands strong and sure on her back.

He stroked one hand all the way up her spine and then all the way down again. "Kissing in public, huh?" he asked.

"And holding hands," she said, lacing her fingers through his and strolling down the block.

"You're really flying in the face of all these rules, you know."

Lexi strolled along with him, hand in hand, too happy, too excited to think twice about her words. "Oh, whatever. The rules don't apply in L.A."

Eric stopped walking and tugged her back against him. "Is that so?"

His words and tone were light, but the way he dragged her against him, the way his eyes suddenly bored into hers, Lexi could see that her words had affected him.

She shrugged and opened her mouth, not sure what to say. Not sure what she *could* say to explain all that she was feeling for him.

* * *

Once they were back in the car, Eric tuned out Lexi and George's conversation about all the different parts of L.A. as he stared out the window and watched it all rush past. *The rules don't apply in L.A.* Her words echoed through his head again and again. What did she mean by that? Did she mean they didn't apply this weekend? Or was she telling him that if they both lived in L.A. they could be together?

He scanned back through all their conversations. Nothing she'd ever said had made it seem like she was intrinsically opposed to relationships. She was just opposed to a relationship that would keep her from her dreams in L.A.

He thought about kissing her on the street corner. Holding her hand.

He watched Echo Park roll past. He'd always liked this neighborhood.

Could he live here?

Maybe. But then images of his ranch flashed through his head and he barely kept from groaning. Yes, he could live here with Lexi, try to beat out a new path in L.A. But no, he couldn't leave his ranch half finished. His *dreams* half finished.

He looked at Lexi, leaning up against the partition and animatedly talking to George.

Quicksand.

For the first time since he'd met her, Eric finally, truly understood her fears.

She could so easily suck him back into L.A. And if she did, no matter how happily he went, it would mean losing a part of himself that he might never be able to get back again.

The rules don't apply in L.A.

Well, this weekend, he would hold tight to that

thought. This weekend, he'd make sure the rules didn't hold them back. They'd have one for the record books. One they could remember fondly as they lived their separate lives in separate parts of the country.

His phone vibrated in his pocket, jolting him out of his depressed reverie. "Hey, Mom."

He listened for a second and then immediately held it out for Lexi to take. "It's for you."

She frowned at the phone, like he was handing her a live grenade. But she took it and held it to her ear. "Hi, Mrs. Davenp—"

Eric grinned as he listened to his mother launch into a long speech about something. Lexi barely had time to make sounds of approval before she was handing the phone up to George. "She wants to talk to you now, George."

"Yo, Mrs. D."

His driver and his mother chatted for a moment while Eric raised his eyebrows in question at Lexi.

Her brow was furrowed and her fingernail had made its way back into her mouth. "Apparently I have a massage and a manicure and pedicure in twenty minutes. Then your mom wants to take me to get my hair done and shopping."

Eric frowned, about to tell her she didn't have to do anything she didn't want to, but then he saw the light of excitement in her eyes. Like last night, she was fighting conflicting feelings. "Is that something you want, Lex?"

She shrugged. "It will be too expensive. Your mom said she wanted to treat me, and I don't want to offend her, but—"

"Don't worry about that, please. My mom doesn't do anything she doesn't want to, and I know she'd love to spend more time with you. But you didn't answer my question. Do *you* want to do all that? Because if you don't..."

She stared at him before speaking. "I think I do. I mean... You know I—I grew up with my father..."

Yes, he did know. During their time at the hardware store, they'd talked a lot about Lexi's childhood, including how her mother had died when she just a baby and how her father had raised her. He knew that Lexi adored her father, and felt guilt that he'd given up his dreams as an actor to give her what she needed. She still felt guilty, given that he was getting on in years and she wished she had the money to help him retire and move on to a simpler, easier life. It was a big part of what motivated her to make it big in L.A., that and the fact that she simply loved movies and writing.

"Go on, Lex," he prompted when she fell into silence.

"I haven't had a mom/daughter day, not in a long, long time. And the fact your mom wants to do all this for me? It's...nice." Her lip trembled, and Eric couldn't help leaning down to kiss her gently.

He rubbed his thumb against her cheek. "Then have a wonderful time, Lex. You deserve it."

They dropped her off at the salon, but not before Lexi leaned across the seat and kissed him again, breathlessly, almost desperately. George let out a long whistle as soon as she was out of earshot.

"Quite a girl you found yourself, Eric."

He could barely bring himself to respond. It wasn't safe to speak until his heartbeat resumed its normal pace. "I know. I want to do something for her this afternoon. You want to drive or you want to take me to my car?"

"An errand for that girl? I'll drive."

13

Lexi looked at herself in the full-length mirror in the bathroom. She'd been buffed, waxed, filed, plucked, smoothed, lotioned, painted, and glossed to within an inch of her life today. Oh, and had her feet jammed into torture devices that Mrs. Davenport had insisted were shoes.

Mrs. Davenport. Just the thought of her had her smiling even as little waves of PTSD rolled through Lexi. She sat down on the edge of the tub to give herself just a minute. She'd bet a hundred bucks that the woman slept standing up.

Lexi's first impressions of her, over the phone, were that she was refined and elegant. And in a lot of ways, she was. Her clothes, her hair, her jewelry. Lovely really. Light brown, like Eric's, and shot through with silver in places. But in person, she was surprisingly relatable and down to earth, even if she was a task master when it came to shopping and beautifying.

"You want to know the secret to walking in heels?"

Mrs. Davenport had asked.

Lexi had nodded, even though she really wasn't sure she wanted to know anything of the kind.

"You never bend your knees. Straight from the hip." She'd showed her what she meant and Lexi had been impressed with the sway in the older woman's walk.

Now, back in the bathroom at the hotel, Lexi rose from the edge of the tub and took another look at herself. Not a runway model, exactly. But a hell of a long way from Lexi Fischer, rodeo baby, broke and blowing in the wind.

Her nails were painted and her legs were a mile long in heels. Her hair was shiny and golden down her back.

"Lovely," her hair stylist had said. "I don't want to change a thing. Except for maybe an inch off the back. And why don't we just give this a gloss."

She hadn't known what the hell a 'gloss' was. But Lexi had to admit, her hair looked amazing. And it perfectly suited Marina's dress. It was a bit snugger on Lexi than it probably was on Marina, straight across the top, with only Lexi's breasts to add some curve to it. And curve they did. The bra Mrs. Davenport had helped her pick out was a masterpiece. The thin, thin straps of the dress swept the material into a long sweep down her legs that would have been conservative if not for the slit up the one leg that came almost to Lexi's hip.

Lexi had to admit, the sky high black pumps with the red sole were the perfect addition. She'd been very uncomfortable with the fact that Mrs. Davenport had insisted on purchasing them, but there was really no saying no to that woman.

Lexi took a deep breath and prepared to go out and face Eric when her phone gave a little buzz on the bathroom counter.

Lexi couldn't help but laugh at the text from Mrs. Davenport.

-Remember dear, just a touch of the mascara. And use that lipstick I got for you. Just a little something to make that pout pop.

Lexi dutifully followed directions and the illusion was complete. She was fit to be Eric Davenport's date to a gala.

Who'd have thunk it.

She took a deep breath and swung open the bathroom door. Stepping out into the living area of the hotel suite, Lexi swung around at a crashing sound.

Eric was standing on the other side of the room in a smart, black tux, his bow tie was undone, lying flat in two straps on his chest. His hair was perfectly trimmed, and his mouth was open as he looked her up and down. He shook his head once, twice, and Lexi had time to look around and realize that he must have knocked over the fruit basket on the table when he'd first seen her.

It went a long way toward boosting her confidence.

"Holy god, Lex." He crossed the room toward her. "You look… You look... Jesus. You look like a goddess."

She blushed. "Thank you. And *you* look like James Bond."

Eric grinned and shoved his hands in his pockets when he got within reaching distance of her. She'd rather he'd grabbed her and kissed her. He was making her all nervous.

"Well, now that we've sufficiently drooled over one another," she said, "are you ready for this thing?" She cocked out one elbow for him to take but he shook his head.

"Not yet. I haven't sufficiently drooled over you yet." Eric reached into the pocket of his coat and pulled out a long, thin box.

Lexi's throat closed and panic rose up inside her. This was how she'd felt last night when she'd first seen this monstrosity of a hotel room. Raw anxiety. Money did this to her. She just wasn't comfortable with it.

She took a step back from him.

"Relax, Lex," he said with a smile. "I know better than to get you fancy jewelry. Trust me. It's a bauble. Really. You could have bought it for yourself. I just saw it and thought of you."

More intrigued than terrified now, Lexi held her hand out for the box and sucked in a delighted breath when she opened it up. Inside was a simple silver chain with two little charms on it. A small black, shiny stone, and dainty silver outline of Montana. So small you might not even realize what it was if you weren't looking for it.

Lexi grinned up at Eric as she pulled it out of the box. "I love it."

"I thought you might."

* * *

Lexi was too busy putting the necklace on, checking it out in the mirror to see the sad smile on his face.

Eric watched the silver charm settle against her collarbone. A little bit above her heart, but close enough. He hoped she'd wear it and think of him. He also hoped she'd never find out that the black stone was actually a black diamond and cost more than her entire summer's wages. She'd skin him alive.

But he'd wanted her to have it. And it looked so right on her, just as he'd known it would.

"Alright," he said as he cocked an elbow out to her the way she'd done to him moments before. "Now we're ready. Let's get outta here before we're late and my mother turns us into shish kabobs."

* * *

"Eric," Lexi said as they rode in the elevator up to the gala. He'd told her it was on the top floor of some fancy building with an amazing view. With each floor they passed, Lexi felt anxiety ripple through her in ever-increasing waves. Eric was her lifeline. So strong and warm and real and handsome right next to her. She knew it might not be fair, but needed to lean on him.

"Hmm?" he asked, brushing her hair back from her shoulder.

"Maybe tonight. Just for tonight, you could introduce me as your girlfriend?"

His eyes were the darkest she'd ever seen them. Almost a midnight blue. For a moment, Lexi wondered if she'd made a mistake in asking. Then he smiled gently. "Of course, Lex. Whatever you want."

Cool. So maybe not such a big deal after all. And it was just the additional piece of armor Lexi felt she needed to walk into the cavernous room that opened up before them as the elevator doors slid to the side.

"Jesus Christ," she muttered to herself. "Everybody is so... glittery."

Eric chuckled. "That does seem to be the goal around here."

And that was the last thing he said to her before they were swallowed up in the crowd.

"Eric! Long time no see."

"Davenport, you dog. Where have you been hiding this beautiful woman?"

"Eric, I wonder if I might have a moment of your time?"

"Eric, have you sampled the wine yet, it's from my brother-in-law's vineyard. If you like it, I wonder if you might want to take this lovely woman on a trip to see it sometime? An investment opportunity perhaps?"

"Davenport, I've been wondering when you'd resurface. Are you done hiding in east of nowhere?"

Twenty minutes later, when the crowd thinned a bit, Lexi tugged Eric into a side hallway that she was pretty sure was reserved for the staff. Whatever.

"These people are awful!" she hissed at him, involuntarily straightening his tie and smoothing her hands down the arms of his jacket. "How can you even stand this?"

Eric cleared his throat and played with the charm at her neck. "I gotta say, it's a lot easier with you at my side. But they're not all awful, Lexi. I have good friends here, too. People who—"

"Eric?"

If Lexi hadn't been able to guess who the gorgeous woman calling his name was, a big clue would have been the way he stiffened in her arms and the way his eyes went cautious.

He turned to the beautiful brunette, her hair in a classic Hollywood pinup style, her curvaceous body highlighted to perfection in her lavender dress. "Brianne."

He hesitated only a split second before stepping into her hug. Lexi watched him carefully, but she didn't see yearning or remorse in his expression. In fact, the smile he gave Brianne seemed genuine, as did the smile Brianne gave him, though Lexi also saw relief in the other woman's expression, as well.

Brianne looked her way. "Hello," she said to Lexi. "I'm Brianne."

"Hi."

"Brianne, this is Lexi. My girlfriend."

Brianne's eyes went wide for just a second. But it was nothing compared to the way Lexi's heart expanded in her chest. She'd requested the title. She knew that of course. But she hadn't expected the way it would make her feel to have Eric say it. To have his deep, perfect voice say that word and be talking about her.

"It's so nice to meet you." Brianne stepped forward and to Lexi's surprise, enfolded her in a quick but tight hug. Just as Brianne pulled back, a huge, dark-haired man came up behind her and placed a hand on her shoulder. "Eric," he said quietly.

This must be Gabe. Figured that he'd be good looking too. Lexi pursed her lips and looked him up and down. Eric had insisted there weren't hard feelings over his best friend stealing his fiancée. But still, just for good measure, she wanted these strangers to know exactly whose team she was on.

"Gabe," Eric said. And then he moved forward and embraced his friend, just like Brianne had embraced Lexi. "It's good to see you."

Gabe pounded Eric on the back, and his expression, like Brianne's, also held no small measure of relief. They loved each other. But they also loved Eric, Lexi realized. They cherished his friendship. And that went a long way toward making her feel less defensive around them.

But still. She couldn't help but give them a little bit of a hard time.

When Gabe turned toward her, she said, "I'm Eric's girlfriend. How do you two know Eric?"

Gabe and Brianne looked surprised. Horrified even.

Eric and Lexi burst out laughing.

"I'm sorry," Lexi chuckled. "I had to."

Smiles crept onto Brianne and Gabe's faces as they realized she was just giving them a hard time. And as they realized that Eric was laughing his ass off.

"So," Brianne said, her blush fading from her cheeks. "You guys are really right out in the lion's den here. Why don't you come to the balcony? It's a friendlier crowd out there. Jamie and Lucy. And a couple of magic men from Vegas."

Eric stopped walking. "You're kidding. Max and Rhys?"

Brianne nodded in true delight. "And Grace and Melina, of course."

Before they stepped onto the balcony, Eric swiped a glass of champagne from a tray and handed it to Lexi. "These are the good people I was telling you about. I can't wait for you to meet them."

"Eric!"

"Davenport!"

His name rang out with genuine affection. He was passed around the group. Hugs and handshakes from the men, and kisses from the women.

"This is my girlfriend, Lexi," he called out to the group. She half smiled and executed a little wave. "This is Jamie and Lucy." He pointed to a gorgeous dark-haired man and a stunning redhead in a short emerald green dress and purple heels. Then he gestured to two couples, a sexy set of identical twins, one with a pretty dark-haired woman, and the other with a beautiful blonde. "These are

Rhys and Melina, and Max and Grace."

"Oh!" Lexi's eyes widened. "I've seen your act in Vegas."

Rhys and Max were celebrity magicians and she'd been able to catch their show a few years ago in Vegas.

They both smiled. "You live in Vegas?" Max asked.

"Nah," she shook her head. "I used to rodeo and the circuit took us just west of there. A few of us came in for the show one night."

"That's awesome. So you were on the rodeo circuit? Tell us more."

* * *

Across the balcony, Eric watched Lexi laugh with his friends and thought how well she seemed to be fitting in.

"She's lovely," a familiar voice said in his ear.

Eric turned to see Dante Callaghan, a former business colleague. Eric grinned and shook the man's hand. "Great to see you, Dante. You still doing business with Gio?"

"Pretty regularly, yes."

"I haven't seen him."

"Look for a pretty redhead and your chances will increase dramatically."

Eric cocked a brow. "That so? Someone special?"

"Seems so."

"I never thought I'd see the day a woman tamed Gio. Shit, she must be something special."

Dante's gaze shifted to Lexi, his meaning clear. Eric

stared at Lexi a moment, taking in all that was her, before he nodded. "She's definitely someone special," he confirmed.

"Yet I sense something's weighing on you."

Eric shrugged. "She's coming back to live here in August. I'm not." His mouth suddenly dry, he took a big swallow of champagne. "This... the two of us here together... it's just temporary. To her, I'm quicksand."

"And to you?"

"To me, she's..." Everything. She's everything to me, he wanted to say. Instead, he simply said, "To me, she's whatever she'll give me in the time we have left together."

"Right. Well I hope it all works out for you. I know you're in Montana now, but if you—" Whatever Dante was going to say next was cut off as the other man stiffened and his gaze became hyper-focused. Turning, Eric followed his line of sight to where a beautiful woman was standing inside. It was Aurora LeMonde, Gio Esposito's executive assistant. She was wearing a figure-hugging red dress that showcased her curves to perfection and although she smiled and greeted those who walked past her, it was clear her attention was focused on a couple across the room: Gio Esposito and a pretty redhead.

Shit, she was in love with Gio and she looked heartbroken, Eric thought, but he wondered if it was only because of his own conflicted feelings for Lexi that Eric could see that.

"Dante—" Eric began, but when he looked back at the other man, Eric's mouth shut with an audible click. Maybe it wasn't heartbreak, but there was yearning on Dante's face. Yearning for Aurora LeMonde.

Shit, this place was just filled with the pain of unrequited love, wasn't it?

Eric's gaze had once again found Lexi when Dante slapped him on the shoulder.

"It was good talking to you, Eric, but I see someone I need to speak with. I hope things work out for you and Lexi," he said, and then he was gone.

Eric watched as Dante approached Aurora. He took a moment to mentally wish Dante the same luck the man had just wished Eric, but then he spotted another familiar face in the crowd inside.

Quickly, Eric walked to Lexi, said some hurried goodbyes, and tugged her inside.

"Hey! I was talking with Grace!" Lexi protested. But Eric grabbed another glass of champagne, shoved it into her hands and brought her face to face with the handsome silver-haired man he'd spotted.

"Lexi, I'd like for you to meet Porter Ford."

He quickly shook hands with the Oscar-winning screenwriter, even though they'd just seen one another that afternoon.

Lexi's eyes were big as saucers and apparently her mouth wasn't working anymore. Maybe he should have warned her before he'd sprung the intro on her. But he hadn't wanted her to get nervous.

Eric nudged her in the side.

"I…wow… God." Lexi held out her hand.

"I usually love for a pretty woman to refer to me as her God. But how about we just leave it at Porter." Porter winked at her and took her hand in his.

Eric could have done with a little less flirting, but whatever got her in the door.

Well, certainly not *whatever*.

"I've been looking forward to meeting you all day," Porter said, finally dropping her hand.

Lexi squinted her eyes in confusion. "You have?"

"Yes, ever since Davenport dropped off your manuscript with me this afternoon."

Lexi's eyes found his. "He did?"

"I didn't want to get your hopes up. Or freak you out." Eric shrugged. "But Porter texted me an hour ago to say that he'd read it and was really impressed."

Lexi looked once again at the other man. "You were?"

"That's right. If you're interested, I'd like to mentor you when you make the move to L.A."

Lexi, apparently, had run out of words.

"You show real talent. There are some classes I'd like for you to take. And when you're ready, I think you'd make a great addition to my writer's group. What do you say?"

When she was still standing there like a fish on dry land, Eric leaned in to whisper in her ear. "Say yes, Lex."

"Yes," she repeated dimly. "Yes, absolutely. I'd love that."

"Great." Porter smiled at someone over Eric's shoulder. "Davenport will keep us in touch. Good luck with your move."

Porter moved away and that was all the warning Eric got before he was drowning in Lexi's kiss.

14

By the time Lexi and Eric were in the elevator back up to their hotel room, she was sagging against his shoulder. It had been quite the night. Drinks and dinner and dancing. He hadn't been surprised to learn that she was a good dancer. Unschooled, maybe. But natural.

The same way she was with everything. A true natural talent.

He hadn't been able to take his eyes off her.

God, he was so screwed.

Tomorrow they were going to fly back to Montana and go back to what? Friends with benefits? That was if he was lucky. Another month of that and then Bye Bye Birdy.

The thought curdled in his stomach.

He held her around the waist as he unlocked the door. She immediately shucked off her shoes as he slid his tie off and laid his jacket over a chair.

"That was really fun," she murmured.

She was tired enough that Eric assumed that sex was

off the table for the night. In a way, he was almost relieved. He didn't think his stupid, hopeful heart could take it right now. He'd take the couch. Keep things a little simpler between the two of them. He slid his shirt out from his pants and started unbuttoning.

"The gala was alright. But the rest was really nice."

"The rest?" she asked from behind him. He could hear her rustling around and getting undressed.

"Yeah," he said, deciding to be honest. "Pretending you were my girlfriend for the night. It was really nice." He stripped off his shirt and lowered his hand to his pants, then thought better of it.

"Eric," she said from behind him. And when he turned to look at her, his heart literally stopped. She stunned in black lace, her silk dress in a pool at her feet. She drew back the covers on the giant king sized bed and looked back over her shoulder at him. "The night's not over."

He was next to her in a second. Less than. But he vowed to himself that that was the last time he was going to go fast tonight. Tonight was about savoring her. Every last drop. She was the finest whisky. The darkest chocolate. The ripest fruit. He wasn't going to let a single taste go to waste.

Sweeping the hair up off her neck, Eric buried his nose in her skin, couldn't get enough of her natural scent.

"You were the only woman in there who wasn't bathed in perfume," he murmured against her, his lips dragging over her skin. "And you smelled better than any of them."

Her breath caught as his hand scraped up her thigh, his fingers twisting in the lace of her panties.

The rules don't apply in L.A.

Throwing every single plan to distance himself out the window, Eric stripped her of the black lace that, while sexy as fuck, didn't hold a candle to the beauty of her naked skin. I can't deny myself this, he thought.

I can't deny myself of a single second with her.

Maybe it would torture him in the morning, when they pulled away from one another. But he couldn't resist. Couldn't resist showing both of them what could have been.

* * *

Eric's hands were large and strong, and they moved over Lexi's body as carefully and reverently as if she was a fine piece of art. Her body tingled as he gently massaged and kneaded and explored every square inch of her before finally concentrating on the very center of her, drawing hoarse moans from her throat and causing shockwave after shockwave of pleasure to ripple through her.

She reached for his pants, yearning to touch him, desperately wanting to see his rock hard abs, grab his incredibly firm ass, and feel his long, stiff cock in her hands. To her surprise and immense frustration, he stopped her. "Not yet, Lexi. You'll have your turn. Right now I need to taste you again," he said, pushing her thighs apart as he lowered his face between her legs. The warmth of his breath upon her opening hit her hard, but it was the tip of his tongue, which he used to circle her clit before diving in deeper, that really made her toes curl. She gasped and moaned, burying her fingers into his hair as Eric worked his magic, slow and steady, as if they had all night to explore each other's bodies. Her back arched up from the bed as he buried his tongue inside of her and she moaned so loud, it echoed off the walls of the bedroom.

Grabbing his head, she ground her pussy against his warm, wet mouth. He sucked and licked and fucked her with his tongue, bringing her close to the edge before slowing his pace and bringing her back down.

She whimpered in disappointment, drawing a devious little smile from him as he looked up at her, her juices glistening on his face. The sight sent chills through her body, and made the fire inside her burn even brighter.

"Fuck me. Fuck me, please," she pleaded after he'd brought her a third time, and then fourth time, to the edge, only to pull her back.

At her hoarse pleas, Eric stood and slowly removed his shirt. Then his pants. When he was naked, she smiled. "My turn now."

She leaned forward and kissed his chest even as she took his cock in her hand. He watched her, a look of pure lust shining brightly in his eyes, as she lowered her face, finally sucking the tip of his cock between her lips. She played there for several minutes before taking more of him. Yes! He filled her mouth so thoroughly and completely, and she shuddered with anticipation and the knowledge of what it would feel like when he filled up other parts of her body.

Eric tangled his fingers into her hair and she sucked and licked him harder, faster, her hand jerking him off in time with her mouth. He moaned, his breathing growing ragged. He was clearly enjoying her mouth on his cock, but she didn't want to finish him like this. No, she needed to fuck him, needed to feel him inside her pussy.

"Please, Eric... Please..."

He suddenly pulled her to her feet beside the bed and kissed her long and hard. Taking one of her breasts in his hand, he gently sucked on the nipple, causing her to squirm and cry out. The feeling of that hard, thick cock pressed into her flesh was driving her mad. She so badly wanted to guide it inside of her, to feel him stretching her open. To feel that long, hard dick plumbing the depths of her. But he continued teasing, spreading her legs and rubbing the head of his cock up against her clit, sending electrical signals throughout her entire body. She closed her eyes and let out a whimper. She felt like a person dying of thirst, laying there on the ground, with a glass of life-saving water sitting just out of her reach.

"Please, please—"

The tip of his cock pressed against her opening, gently parting her lips, as he stared down into her eyes. His blue eyes were like oceans of lust, and she felt like she was drowning in them. God, he was so damn sexy and he was so close to giving her what she wanted. What she needed. He was so goddamn close to fucking her and she was crying out for him to slide his cock inside her.

She arched her back upward, hoping to seal the deal and join their two bodies. But he suddenly pulled back with a curse. "Protection," he said, quickly finding a condom and putting it on. When he was back, a life-saving glass of water out of reach, she whimpered. "Easy. I've got you." He smiled, pressing against her again, this time allowing just the tip of his glorious cock to fill her.

"No need to rush. I want to savor this, Lexi. I want to savor every last bit of you," he said quietly, kissing her. "Because God knows, once I'm inside of you, I won't be able to control myself."

"Then lose control, Eric," she said softly, stroking his cheek. "Please, lose control. I want you to."

He looked down at her for a long moment, the aching in her body intensifying with each passing second. She thought that he was going to prolong her suffering by making her wait, but he took her by complete surprise when he thrust himself deep inside her. She dug her nails into his shoulders, hanging on for dear life as he filled her up, going deeper than she thought possible. Her eyes were wide and a strangled gasp escaped her lips as he stretched her wide open.

As their bodies came together, they both let out a groan of pleasure, and she felt herself clenching around his cock.

He moved slowly at first, rocking back and forth, sliding his cock in and out of her with no sense of the desperation she felt. He was content to stare down into her eyes as he slowly fucked her. Each thrust inside of her felt amazing. Her body tingled like she was being zapped with electricity, and she knew it wouldn't be long for either of them.

Eric's body began to tremble and he started pumping his cock into her faster and harder. He was growing more and more desperate, and closer to climax. As was she. She could feel it building up inside of her – like a wave out on the ocean that was gaining speed and strength as it approached the shore. She had a feeling that when the wave finally broke, it was going to shake her to her very core.

The spasms started low in her pussy, making her clench around his cock even tighter. Eric squeezed his eyes shut harder as he let out a low groan.

"Oh fuck," he muttered under his breath, shuddering against her as she continued tightening around him.

She wrapped her arms around his body, holding him close, and she arched herself upward to meet his thrusts. And then – well, then she lost it. That wave out on the ocean came crashing down, forcing her to lose control of her body – and her mind, really – and let out a scream, calling out his name as wave after wave of pleasure overcame her.

With her squirming and writhing underneath him like a wild animal, he had a hard time keeping the rhythm, but somehow, he was able to manage. At least, he managed to keep the rhythm until the last wave of pleasure crashed down upon her and that was apparently all he needed.

"Lexi... Oh God..." He thrust into her one last time, deep enough to hit her cervix, and let out a low grunt.

She cried out as his cock pulsed inside her one last time. He squeezed his eyes shut as he exploded. Immediately, she joined him in orgasm – the two of them shuddering and writhing, their bodies grinding against one another as they rode out the pleasure together.

* * *

Lexi came awake the next morning like a patient waking from a coma. She had absolutely no sense of time or place. The only thing she knew was warmth. And safety. And something else. Something hot and light and burning inside her.

What was that feeling? She'd never felt it before. It was halfway between mania and calm. Panic and joy.

Without opening her eyes, Lexi moved her hand to her heart. But found that someone else's hand was already there.

Her eyes sprang open.

Eric.

He was spooned around her, one hand clutching the charm he'd given her last night. The rest of the night washed over her. The dress. The friends. Brianne and Gabe, and Porter, and Eric. Oh god, Eric. Dancing. Laughing.

Making love.

Unlike anything she'd ever experienced in her life.

Eric had opened her up like a Christmas present. Lit her on fire from the inside.

Every kiss, every moan, every delicious, languid stroke of him inside her was burned into her brain.

They'd made love on the bed. Over and over again. He'd stoked the flame for hours. They'd been a tangle of wanting limbs, trying to climb inside one another.

She realized now, with a kind of fascinated horror, that they'd been trying to bind themselves to one another.

Jesus God. That had not been sex. That had been love.

And that feeling tearing its way out of her chest? That was love.

Lexi moved her hand over her open, horrified mouth. What the fuck had she done? She'd fallen in love?

Somewhere between the hardware store and the fancy ass gala, Lexi had gotten herself good and lost. This was brand new country. Fresh territory that she had absolutely no interest in fording.

She was screwed. She was utterly screwed. Because best case scenario? Eric didn't feel the same way back. He would be so sweet about it. Let her down gently. With class and kindness. The thought made her stomach completely clench.

And worst case scenario? He felt the same way that she did. Instantly Lexi was bombarded with images of herself sitting on the front porch on Eric's ranch. Kids playing in the yard and horses galloping in the paddock.

It was a beautiful image. A beautiful life. And she wanted it. Desperately.

Only she couldn't have it. Not without giving up her dream. Not without giving up herself, the way her father had given up himself to do the right thing by Lexi and her mother.

She couldn't do that. No matter how much she longed to be with Eric, she couldn't let herself be mired in quicksand.

Lexi slid out from under Eric's arm. Cursing herself for what she'd done. What she'd allowed to happen.

She shook her head as she dug into her bag for her regular clothes. No. No sense beating herself up over that. It was bound to happen at some point no matter what she did. The fact was, she'd been screwed the second Eric had sat down next to her at the bar. She'd never stood a chance against that grin. Those eyes. That delicious, deep voice.

No! Concentrate! She dressed quickly and packed her things as quietly as she could.

She indulged herself in just one more look at Eric. And then she stepped out onto the balcony and made the first phone call.

"Jake? Hi. It's Lexi."

* * *

Eric woke up that morning feeling like he could run a marathon. No. Better than that. He could win a marathon right about now. His muscles were warm and loose. His body rested. And his skin still tingled from the hours long sexcapade he'd had with Lexi.

He'd never had sex like that. Where the heat from their bodies made it feel like they were melting together. He'd swallowed down her breath. Every moan and gasp. He'd fucked her hard. And soft. And everything in between. Drawn it out so long that the last twenty minutes had just felt like one long orgasm.

Seriously. There was no recovering from that. Once you knew sex like that existed, you didn't go back to get-to-know-you sex.

He stretched and reached out for her. He was only partially surprised to feel that she wasn't in the bed.

He was ready for whatever freak out she was going to send his way this morning. It was a par for the course reaction of hers whenever they got closer. He was fine with it, really. She'd set some more rules. He'd accept them, and then they'd head back to Montana. Try to take things easy for a while.

He was fine with that. Especially now that he knew they could have sex like that. Sex where he got to tell her every single thing he was feeling without even having to say a word. He figured she wouldn't be able to keep him at arm's length for too long if they were fucking like that every night.

So he took it on the chin when he sat up and didn't see her in the room. She needed a little space. That was fine. But his brow furrowed when he saw that she wasn't in the bathroom either.

He was brushing his teeth when she stepped back in from the balcony. She was tucking her cell phone into her jeans pocket. She was already dressed for the day? Mildly disappointed, he rinsed his toothbrush. He'd been looking forward to lazing around in bed for an hour or two before they got back out to see more of L.A.

"Morning," he said, trying not to be hurt when she avoided his eye. "Who were you talking to out there?"

She took a deep breath, sat down at the breakfast table and turned to face him. "A few people."

He sat down next to her, grabbed an orange and started to peel it. "Oh? Who?"

"Jake, Aubrey, and Marina."

Eric was starting to get a sick feeling in his stomach. "In that order?"

"Yes."

Eric tossed the orange aside. "What's this about, Lex?"

She took another deep breath. "I'm staying here."

Eric stared her in the eye as her words sank down on him, one after the other. "You mean—"

"I'm not coming back to Montana."

He leaned back in his chair suddenly feeling like he was the one who needed distance.

"I talked with Jake first," she plunged on. "Because I wanted to make sure that he could help you out at the hardware store for a few hours a day for the next month. I didn't want to leave you high and dry."

"Jake doesn't have time to—"

"Well, he said he'd do it. Because I need him to."

That shut him up.

"And then I talked to Aubrey. Asked if I could move in today. He said yes. He was stoked actually. And then I talked to Marina. I'm going to wire her rent for the next month, because I know she was depending on it. And she's going to ship me the stuff I left in Montana. Although, honestly, there's not much left. Except for my car. Which she said she'd try and sell for me."

Eric felt a huge hole opening up inside of him, yawning and scratching to get at every last inch of his heart. "That must have been a hard conversation, I know you two are friends." His voice was hollow, even to his own ears.

"It was. But she understood."

Suddenly Eric was standing, pacing away from her. "What did she understand exactly?"

Lexi rose too. Her eyes were steady but her voice was not. "That if I go back, Eric, if I go back with you, I'll never leave."

"Lexi—"

"No! Listen." She raced forward and took his hand. Broke his heart when she placed it against her own cheek. "Eric, you're too good. You're worth it. You're worth staying in Montana for. But it'll wreck me to do it. And I can't do that to myself. I'll never forgive myself if that's the choice I make. Never."

"Long distance," he tried.

"With no end in sight? You really want that?"

"No." Yes? He had no fucking clue what he wanted. All he knew was that this felt terrible. Like he was tearing himself in half.

"So why drag it out? Why pile on another month of closeness just to have to kick our way out of it at the end? No way. This is hard enough as it is. And I've only loved you for like ten hours. I can't imagine what it would be like at the end of the summer."

His eyes snapped up to hers. His hands were on her shoulders. "You love me?"

She met his gaze, but it was with sadness, resignation. "Does it matter? Does it really change anything?"

He wanted to shake her. Wanted to shake himself. Slap himself. Become a different man who wouldn't hate himself for returning to L.A. with his tail between his legs.

"Does it change anything if I love you back?" he asked, wanting the one answer that he knew he was never going to get.

"Don't," she whispered, her chin trembling. "This is hard enough without both of us telling the fucking truth."

"You knew?" He had to know. "You knew how I felt?"

She threw up her hands and took a step away from him. And then another step. "It's written all over us, Eric."

He watched as she took another step and another step. She reached for her neatly packed backpack.

"If you're ever in L.A..." she started.

"Don't say it."

So she didn't. She gave him one last look, halfway between tough and heartbroken. And then the door of the hotel room was clicking shut behind her.

15

Well, the good part about being heartbroken as hell was that he didn't have to bother with sleep anymore. And as a result, he was almost three quarters of the way toward having a fully operational horse ranch.

It had been a month since he'd left Lexi in L.A. A month since they'd spoken, and in a way, it soothed him that it was August 1st. This was always going to be the date that he lost her. He was going to end up being heartbroken on August 1st no matter how he'd played it. The inevitability of it was almost a balm. There was nothing he could do. Nothing he could have ever done. No other cards he could have pulled. She was just as gone as she always was.

The woman that had captivated him from the beginning. Tough and nervous. Sweet and prickly. Childlike and world worn. Gone as she always was. Even when he had her.

Eric took a big swig of beer, even though it was just

pushing 11 am, and looked out over his land. He had two horses in the paddock. One of them sniffed at the hay and the other was appreciating the shade inside his barn.

He tore his eyes from the new structure. He didn't like to remember the sound of a mallet hitting the wall. The sound of Lexi smashing her way through whatever she had to in order to let herself touch him that night.

"Eric."

Eric started at the sound of Jake's voice. He hadn't heard a car pull up.

Jake bounded up the porch steps. "Drinking kind of early don't you think?"

"I didn't hear you drive up."

"You were lost in thought, looked like."

"Everything alright at the store?" It embarrassed Eric to know it, but he'd completely disconnected from his grandparents' store. Pretty much the minute he'd come back, Jake and Dylan had taken over for him. It had just sucked too much to go back there. He'd needed the distraction of his ranch.

"Sure, sure. Your grandparents will be back in a week it sounds like. To be honest, I'll kind of miss it. Sarah Burn sure loves to frequent that shop."

"She have another lamp that needs fixing?" Eric asked, a ghost of a smile on his face.

"Among other things." Jake waggled his eyebrows and made Eric outright laugh for the first time in a month. Jake snagged the beer out of Eric's hands and took a long, healthy swig. "So you did it, man. You got your ranch."

Eric looked out over everything. There was still a lot to do. A lot of things that he supposed were only mostly finished. But yeah. Where it counted, he'd done it. "Suppose you're right."

"So when you headed back to L.A., then?" Jake asked.

Eric started and turned to stare at his friend. "What do you mean?"

"I mean, you wanted to start a ranch. You did it. Now you have another dream to pursue."

Eric shook his head. "I wanted to run a ranch, Jake. Not just start one. I can't run it if I'm in L.A."

"Ah. Well, you got friends, don't you?"

"Friends that would run the whole damn operation while I'm off living a separate life? I don't think so, Jake. The hardware store is one thing. But this? This is something else."

"Well," Jake started, using the same ornery tone as before. "What good is being a billionaire if you aren't going to spend any of that dough? Can't you hire somebody to run this thing for you?"

Eric bit back his irritation. "The whole point was that I run it myself. I'm sick of making my money work for me. I want to do the work." He patted his own chest to make the point.

Jake grabbed onto the rail of the porch and leaned his weight backwards. "Well, you did the damn work, didn't you? You built yourself a goddamn horse ranch in less than three months, didn't you? Did most of the work in the last thirty days. Using nothing but blood, sweat, and what I assume are the many, many tears of a heartbroken man."

Eric sighed but said nothing.

Jake continued on. "If you're going to be suffering this much, you better ask yourself what you're trying to prove and who the hell you're trying to prove it to."

"You don't think I've been asking myself that shit since the day she left?"

"Well what's the answer then?" Jake threw his hands up in exasperation.

"I have to prove it to myself, Jake. In L.A., everybody weighs me by my bank account. But money has no value to your heart. To your spirit. After Brianne and I fell apart, I woke up and I just didn't know how to measure myself anymore. My own worth. All I knew was that I needed a simpler life. Filled with hard work and small, reliable rewards. I was going to lose myself otherwise."

"Jesus Christ," Jake dropped his head in his hands. "I love you, Eric. But these are rich kid problems." He raised his hands in self defense. "Problems nonetheless. Of course. We can't compare pain, yadda yadda yadda. But from where I'm standing, here you are, holding a big rubber stamp in one hand. You know what that stamp says? It says 'success' on it. And all you have to do is this." Jake took Eric's hand and pressed it to Eric's forehead. "Quit torturing yourself and give yourself the label already. You done did it. Success." He released Eric's hand.

"That easy, huh?"

"Hell no. That shit is hard as hell. Trust me. But you know what oughtta be easier than living without her?"

"What's that?"

"Getting out of your own way so you can figure out how to live *with* her."

* * *

Lexi bounded down the steps of the community college where she was taking a few general education courses to ease herself back into school mode. Thankfully, she was doing better than keeping up, she was acing everything so far. In addition, even though she was only making minimum wage working at a coffee shop around the corner from her house, she'd applied for and received a scholarship. As such, she was not only paying all her bills, she was even saving up for a car.

Finally, she was meeting with a writer's group twice a week. It had only been a month and she was already halfway through her second manuscript. It was even better than the first, and she already had ideas for more scripts.

Yes, indeed, she'd made the right decision coming to L.A. It was the best thing she could have done for herself.

And the fact she had to keep telling herself this every few hours didn't mean a thing.

Twenty minutes later, she was unlocking her front door, calling out a hello to Aubrey, who was doing dishes in their kitchen, and then locking herself in her room.

She took a deep breath and lowered herself to her bed

just as her face crumpled.

This happened everyday like clockwork.

While she was busy, out in the world, moving and shaking, she was fine. Good even. Juiced by the simple fact that she was making her dreams come true.

But the second she was alone, the very second, she crumbled in on herself. So homesick for Eric she could barely breathe.

She was homesick for Montana and the friends she'd made there, as well.

The pain should have been easing by now, but it wasn't. If anything, it was worsening. She missed Eric more than she thought possible. Down to the bone. Even her stupid teeth missed Eric.

When she'd given herself a solid twenty minutes of wallowing, Lexi sat up, brushed her hand over her face and reached for her phone. She always felt better after talking to Marina.

She'd just started to dial when someone knocked on her door.

"Lexi?" Aubrey called. "There's an extremely handsome man here for you."

Lexi was off the bed like a shot. Eric. It had to be. A visit? Could she handle it? Could she handle turning him away? Hell no. She already knew she was going to take what she could get. After a month of wallowing, she was ready to torture herself with however much of him he was willing to give.

But when she flung open the door of her bedroom and

bounded into the living room, it wasn't Eric waiting for her.

"Papa!" she yelped, and was in his arms before she could think twice.

"Hey there, baby girl." His grin was bigger than a full moon.

Twenty minutes later they were walking through Chinatown together.

"You've got more gray in your hair, Papa," she teased him. Her eyes dropped down to the leg he was favoring. "And a little hitch in your giddy up."

"Yep. Doctor says I need a new hip."

Lexi stopped walking, earning a dirty look from the business woman rushing along behind her. "You have a fall?"

"Nah. Just your normal wear and tear. Rodeo's a hard life. You know that, baby girl."

"Sure." She was already recalculating her wages, trying to find a way to cover the cost of a surgery like that. Nothing doing. Her car was going to have to wait. She might need to move to a cheaper place. Well, those were the breaks.

"Now, quit that," her father reprimanded. "You look just like your mother when you're doing money math in your head. Break's my heart a little."

Lexi laughed in surprise. "What do you mean?"

"She was always so concerned about money. She'd have rolled over in her grave to know I got us wrapped up in rodeo after she passed. Money pit is what it was."

"I never had any complaints about it," Lexi shrugged. "Makes for good party conversation these days," she teased him. "These L.A. rich kids can't get enough stories about horse country."

He threw his head back and laughed. "Is that right?"

"Yes, sir."

"Well, it wasn't no game to us, now was it?"

"No, sir. That was real life."

"Realer than real," he agreed. Then took a deep breath. "Which is why it was so hard to leave it behind."

"What? Papa? You retired? Is that how you got the time to come visit me?"

"Nah. I made the time to visit you because you're my baby girl living her best life out in Los Angeles. And I'm proud. That's why I come to visit." He scraped a hand over his stubble and looked at her out of the side of his eye. "I ain't got the savings to retire. But I got another job."

"Really? What is it?" Lexi traded cash for two snow cones and handed one to her dad. He chuckled at the electric blue color but took a big bite.

He didn't answer her question about the job, just gave her a long, clear look. "You know you were my biggest dream, right, baby girl?"

"What do you mean, Papa?"

He scrubbed a hand over his stubble. "I mean that you always had it in your head that I woulda been George Clooney if you hadn't come along."

"You're handsome enough."

"Well." He blushed. "Alright. I'm just saying that I

think you always got your dreams confused with mine. You thought I put my hopes on hold to be your daddy. To rodeo. But you got it backwards. The life I lived? That was my best life. What I always wanted. And sure, I was curious about Hollywood. Probably wouldn't have minded starring in a movie or two. But did I want the rest? The pace? The parties? The time away from you? Hell nah."

Lexi tossed her cone in the trash. She'd never heard him speak like this before. She could barely believe her ears.

"Mostly I just told you them stories to keep you entertained. Lord knows I plugged you into movies often enough in the back of that trailer. I think I really just wanted a way to stay involved with you even when I had to be away from you, out working. So I wanted you to picture your daddy in them movies. Dancing and singing and what not. And then after a while, it became your dream. To make movies like that. And I was proud. You was always so creative and smart and such a dreamer. And I'm proud to see you out here in Hollywood, making it happen for yourself."

Lexi felt tears rising and she wasn't altogether sure why.

"But I guess I just wanted to make sure that you weren't getting your dreams mixed up with mine. You know? If this is what you want, then have at it, girl. If this is some sort of vindication for my lost dreams? Well, you can give that up, child. Because I done got my dream. Healthy kid. Good relationship with her. And now I got a good job to settle down with. Stay in one place for a while. I got what I need. What I want."

Lexi was speechless. She wasn't sure if what he'd said was true. If that's the way that she had felt. Whether part of the reason she was out here was because she'd somehow felt like she'd gotten in the way of her father's dreams. But she did know their conversation had made her feel lighter. Like he'd given her permission to let go of a helium balloon she'd been carrying around her whole life. Not exactly a heavy burden, but a burden nonetheless.

"Well, Papa. I guess I just don't know." She wiped a tear from her eye.

"You've got time to figure it out, I suppose," he said, handing her his half finished snow cone. "Here, you done threw yours in the trash when you got upset."

She laughed because he knew her so well. Laughed because she felt light. Laughed because she was happy to be in the same city as her dad.

"Tell me about this new job."

They were halfway back to her house by now, and her father looked at her with a little trepidation in his eye.

"Well, I haven't taken it yet. I wanted to run it by you first."

"Alright," she said, figuring it was some sort of off the books gig he'd want her blessing for.

"It's a ranching gig." His eyes slid sideways to watch her carefully. "Horse ranch. Up in Montana."

Lexi's heart froze but she did her best not to show it. "Is that right?"

"Yup. I'd be working for a young man who knew you by name in fact. An Eric Davenport."

Lexi swallowed hard.

"Boy called me up out of the blue one day 'bout a week ago. Said he had a job offer if I wanted it. Needed someone who knew about horses and who knew about hard work. Figured I knew about both."

"He was right," Lexi choked out. Her mind spinning. What the hell did any of this mean?

"Yep. Well, seems he needs a foreman."

Her face snapped around to his. "I thought he was going to be the foreman."

"Well, seems that's up for debate, depending on the way a few different things shake out. But seems like he's hoping he can be on the ranch a few months a year. And elsewhere a few months a year."

"Elsewhere," she repeated numbly, her heart beating a mile a minute. She missed the little smile from her father.

"So I figured I'd ask you 'fore I took the job."

She cleared her throat. "And why's that?"

"Well, I didn't want to go muckin' up your personal matters between you and this boy you're over the moon for."

"Papa, I'm not—" She broke off since at this point she didn't see the damn point in lying. "He's really great, Papa. The second best man I know." She nudged his wiry old ribs and he smiled.

"Well, seems he's caught a few feelings for you, baby girl."

"He told you that?"

He shrugged. "Didn't have to. Man doesn't rearrange his life for a woman he's on the fence for."

That balloon that Lexi had just let go of? Well, it was currently setting up shop in her belly, expanding to the size of a football field. She felt like she might just lift right off the earth.

She turned to her father. She didn't know in that moment, with blue snow cone on her lips, and her hair back in a ponytail, that she looked more like both a woman and a child than her old dad's heart could bear.

"Papa. Take the job."

16

Eric patted down the old horse that was enjoying the shade of his brand new barn. He was going to miss the smell of the hay and the way the horse chuffed at the morning air. He was going to miss the sun biting through the fog in the morning and falling into bed an exhausted heap every night.

But he wasn't going to miss any of that as much as he missed Lexi.

So the arrangements had been made. He had a new foreman coming next week. He had even more crew coming after that. He'd made sure they'd be comfortable in the guest rooms located in the old farmhouse. There was nothing left to do now but put his heart on the line and see if Lexi wanted the same thing he did.

To be together regardless of how difficult maintaining two homes, two careers, two *dreams*, in two different states might be.

Eric let out a long slow breath and led the horse to her

water. When he heard a car pulling up on his gravel, he figured it was probably Jake ready to give him a kick in the ass again.

Eric patted the old horse on the side then stretched his arms above his head. He was just straightening his ball cap and heading back to his house to meet up with Jake when…

He stopped in his tracks when he saw who was leaning against a cherry red rental car, arms crossed over her chest and one ankle crossed over the other.

Eric took a moment to look at her. The woman who wasn't overly feminine but still more beautiful than any other woman in the word. He adored her lean muscles. Her wild hair. Her tough little face.

"That scowl a permanent fixture on your face?" he called over to her. "Or do you reserve it just for me?"

Lexi turned to him, and he immediately saw the nerves dancing in her eyes. They were easy to spot given his own nerves needed a dancing partner.

"You really did it, Eric." As she straightened, she raised her arms and made an all-encompassing gesture. "And you did it in record time. Have you even slept?"

He was close now, maybe only five feet between them. He felt the pull of her, but couldn't get enough of a read to know how much closer she wanted him. "Not lately."

She bit her lip. "Me either."

"Are you just passing through?" he asked and could have kicked himself for the awkward, stilted way the question had come out.

"I'm not sure," she answered, a very serious expression on her face. "I guess that depends how this visit goes."

His heart knocked on his ribs like it was asking to please come out and play.

"You came to see me."

"I sure did. To ask you a question."

"And what question is that?"

"Why you hired my Daddy to take care of this ranch for half the year."

"Um, well…" Eric scraped a hand over his stubble, eyeing her carefully, like she was a filly who might kick him at any moment. "It appears your father played my cards for me," he grumbled.

Her lips tipped into a small smile. "He wouldn't take a job like that without making sure I was okay with it. So he came to L.A. Spent a few days with me. Spilled your secret."

Eric pictured the slow-talking cowboy he'd spoken with on the phone. Then he tried to picture him in Echo Park. He couldn't help but smile. "How'd he like it?"

She shrugged. "He thought it was interesting. Said he liked Montana better."

"Hmmm. I can't say I disagree with him since you're currently *in* Montana, standing right in front of me."

Lexi stared at him. Then, quick as a cat, she snaked a hand around his belt buckle, and pulled him close until his body pressed hers against the car. The move soothed him and kicked his heart into overdrive. She wanted him closer. But that had never been their problem. Still, he couldn't resist touching her so he slid one hand around the back of her neck, and caressed her bottom lip with the other.

"You want to know why I hired your dad? Because I finally decided to get out of my own way."

"Meaning?"

He took a deep breath and looked around them. At what he'd built. "I thought that in a perfect world, I'd be here 365 days a year. But then I met you. And that's not *your* perfect world. So mine had to change."

"You want to split your time between here and L.A." She whispered the words tentatively, like she might break in two the second they left her mouth.

"I don't know how realistic splitting my time down the middle is, not at first. But I want to spend a lot of time in L.A." He traced his thumb over her bottom lip. "A lot."

"But you hate Los Angeles." She was still whispering. And her eyes were filling with tears. He almost would have preferred her yelling. He'd never seen this lost little side of her before.

He chose his words carefully. "I don't hate L.A. any more than you hate Montana. It's just I wanted Montana to be home so badly, and I thought that meant completely putting aside my life in L.A. I told myself I had to give up my past in order to truly commit to my future. But with you by my side... At the gala... When you met Brianne and Gabe... I never felt like a jilted man with too much money and no purpose returning to the place he'd wanted to leave behind. Instead, I was simply home. Because you're my home, Lexi. Not Montana. Not California. Not any state or city or building. *You*."

Lexi's eyes searched his. Hope and understanding swirled inside her. "So you're really sure? You won't mind regularly visiting me in L.A.?"

He took a deep breath. "No. I want to *live* part-time with you in L.A. And trust your dad to run the ranch whenever I'm not here."

Lexi slammed her eyes shut and dropped her forehead to his chest. He couldn't help but hold his breath.

"I'm working on another screenplay, you know." Her voice was muffled against his chest. "Which I guess makes me a screenwriter. I'm in school for it right now. But we get a summer vacation. And a Christmas break. And a spring break."

Eric felt a hand squeeze over his heart. "Any chance you might want to spend those in Montana?"

Lexi stared at him. Then she shrugged. "No might about it. Because you're my home, too, Eric."

Completely losing his cool at this point, unable to continue this calm charade they had going on, Eric slapped his hands together over his head with a tremendous clap and let out a victory roar. Right before he picked her up and pressed her against the car. Lexi laughed and tilted her head to one side, inviting him to kiss his way up her neck.

They clung to one another, each of them holding their personal successes like burning torches inside them.

They'd taken those first steps. They'd started accomplishing what they'd set out to do and suddenly their path toward one another wasn't quite so murky. They believed in their own ability to shape their lives. And just like that, their lives had room for one another.

They were holding one another so tight they barely had the room to break apart and kiss. Suddenly, Lexi stiffened in his arms, scrambled her way down and started sprinting toward the paddock. "Oh my god!"

She screamed. She jumped up and down. And then she turned and ran back to him. "Eric. You asshole! You absolutely perfect, sweet, considerate asshole."

He laughed as she launched herself right back into his arms.

"You bought back my horse." As she looked back at the paddock, at the horse sniffing at the ground and sauntering through, there were tears in her eyes. "You bought Maple back for me."

"It took some sleuthing, tracking her down, but she was the first horse on my ranch."

Lexi took his mouth in a kiss so soft, so sweet, it was a balm, erasing the pain they'd caused one another over the last month.

She tore her lips away from his and pressed her forehead against his so she stared straight into his eyes.

"You know what this means, don't you?" she asked, almost threateningly.

"What's that?"

"You don't have a choice anymore. You're going to

have to marry me."

Words completely escaped him as his mouth opened and closed like a goldfish.

Lexi threw her head back and laughed, her long, coltish legs wrapped firmly around his waist. "In can be in ten years, I don't care. But you bought my horse back for me. So now we're engaged. The end."

"Damn straight we're engaged. And it's not the end. It's only the beginning."

He dropped his girl to her feet and kissed the ever-loving breath out of her. Took her hand as they walked together toward the paddock. Toward Maple. His land rolled out all around them and somewhere, hundreds of miles away, a city buzzed like a beehive, waiting for them to return.

And even though they'd just decided to live in two places, as messy a plan as it was, for the first time in either of their lives, their hearts were no longer split in two.

EPILOGUE

Lexi and Eric squared off in the living room. Their arms were crossed over their chests, with matching scowls on their faces as they eyed one another like opponents in a boxing ring.

"Absolutely not," Eric said, his voice solid and frustrated. "It's insulting and unnecessary, Lex. No prenup."

"Eric! I'm the one who would be insulted by it and I'm not! I want the damn prenup. I want the most ironclad prenup there is. I'll sign it at the goddamn wedding for all I care. I don't want a single penny of your money."

"It's a moot point, baby. A prenup would only come into play in the event of a divorce, and I am telling you right here and now, I'm not *ever* divorcing you. And you are *never* divorcing me."

"Of course I'm *never* divorcing you." She jabbed a finger into his chest. "If a prenup is a moot point, then let's just have one anyway. That way no one can accuse me of marrying you for your money."

"I don't give a fuck what anyone thinks. I know why you're marrying me. I know it's because you love me. I know it's because you can't live without me, that you don't *want* to live without me, just the way I don't want to live without you."

Lexi's breath hitched. "That's true. That's so true. But Eric, you're a billionaire. And I...I'm not. I'm so far from not. And whether you like it or not, you know your money will be an issue. So let's make it *not* an issue. Please?"

Eric stared at her. Then he cupped her face, kissed her gently, then said, "Okay. Let's make it not an issue."

Relief swept through Lexi before she kissed Eric back. "Thank you," she whispered. Then she frowned when Eric whipped his phone out of his pocket and typed something into it with pointed ferocity.

"What are you doing?" Lexi narrowed her eyes at him and tried to snatch for the phone.

Eric immediately held it up out of her reach and then answered it when it began to ring. "Eric Davenport. Hi, Mr. Rourke. Yes. Yes. I officially authorize it. We did the paperwork on it last month when I was in L.A. I was under the impression that all we needed was the indicator from me that it was time to pull the trigger. Consider the trigger pulled. Yes. I agree. She's not going to be happy." He laughed. "All's fair in love and war. Alright. You bet. Thanks."

He hung up the phone and gave her a triumphant look. "Okay, *now* we can have a prenup drafted."

"What do you mean? What did you do?"

Eric grinned at Lexi, then said, "I just had twenty million dollars transferred into a bank account in your name." He leaned forward and kissed her stunned mouth. "So I'm happy to have a prenup if that's what you want."

"WHAT?! You—" Her mouth open and closed, but she didn't make another sound. Not until she sobbed, flung herself into Eric's arms, and burrowed her face in his chest.

Eric simply stroked her hair and murmured, "Money is just money, Lexi. It will never be a smidgen as important to me as our love. I'd give it all up in a second to be with you. That being said, I'm glad I don't have to. Because I'm going to spoil you. With my body. My heart. *And* our money. Until the day we die. I love you."

Lexi lifted her tear-stained face. "I love you, too, Eric Davenport. Now shut up and kiss me."

He kissed her. He kissed her so long and so passionately that they ended up in the bedroom. And they didn't leave it for a very long time.

Thank you for reading Bedding The Boss.

If you enjoyed spending time with these characters,
be sure to check out Dante and Aurora's story in Book 9,
Bedding The Baby Daddy. Here's a sneak peek!

Excerpt
BEDDING THE BABY DADDY

1

Aurora LeMonde smiled serenely at each guest who passed her, determined to exude confidence and calm at her company's latest fundraising gala even though she felt like she'd swallowed razor blades. She commanded herself not to do it. Not to torture herself. Not to look at him—at *them*—again. Unfortunately, as was too often the case where her boss, Giovanni Esposito, was concerned, Aurora's self-control was nil. Within seconds, she sought him out, spotting him across the room looking like Italian sin in a perfectly tailored suit. He didn't glance her way, his complete attention focused on the redhead by his side.

Whether he knew it or not, Gio was looking down at the love of his life.

Aurora's eyes threatened to fill, her throat closed and everything behind her eyebrows tightened. With the ease of practice, however, she took a deep breath and swallowed her feelings down.

She'd worked for Gio for five years. Lived and breathed him. Loved him hard and quiet.

Convinced herself that at some point, the Universe's cosmic puzzle pieces would fall into place and Gio would walk past her office, see her in the right pencil skirt in the right lighting with the right amount of hair tumbling over her shoulder, and he'd just suddenly… requite.

But she'd missed her chance. Or maybe she'd never had a chance at all. Because all along, a lovely redheaded woman had been living and breathing, and now Gio was looking at her like *that*. As if he'd only just started to exist when she showed up.

So really, Aurora had never had a chance. Not for his heart. Because that look on his face? That was the look of Destiny.

On impulse, Aurora snagged a glass of champagne from a passing waiter and drank the liquid down. Maybe she hadn't had a chance at his heart, but damn, it sure would have been nice to sleep with him a time or two. Something to remember fondly in the old folk's home where she would inevitably die alone.

Not that she was feeling bitter or anything.

She scanned the people around her. She knew most of them, Gio's clients, business associates or friends. There they went, smiling and friendly, some of them gazing at her with warm familiarity, but none of them truly knew her. None of them knew that on the inside she was holding her knees and rocking in a corner. Or that she would leave here and climb into bed alone, just as she always did. She hadn't dated in years. Even flirting with a man had made her feel disloyal to Gio.

She couldn't help but chuckle mirthlessly into her champagne at that one.

She'd been faithful to a man who'd seen her as a sister, a friend, a colleague.

Faithful to a man who'd touched her but never *touched* her. She'd made too much of the occasional tap on the shoulder, or hand to help her into a cab, or a few, glorious times, a victory hug when something had gone right for the firm.

Oh how pathetically she'd burned those moments into her brain.

Aurora took another gulp of champagne and told herself that she only had to give it twenty more minutes here before she could escape. This was a fundraiser for lung cancer research, and many of their clients had donated generously to the cause. There were heavy hitters in attendance, including Los Angeles billionaires Jamie Whitcomb and Eric Davenport, who'd flown in from Montana and his self-imposed exile specifically for this event. She needed to put on a good face and mingle, even if her heart was breaking.

She set her empty champagne glass on a side tray and turned to face the music. Unfortunately, she came face-to-face with George Mills Jr., the son of their oldest client. George was one of the slimiest men Aurora had ever had the misfortune to meet, and she'd had to put up with his leering advances for years. Although she'd been quite clear in her disinterest, he'd shown no signs of giving up the pursuit.

His persistence was rivaled only by one other man's, a business colleague who'd made his interest in Aurora very clear, as well. Only *that* man was far from slimy.

A perpetual, incorrigible suitor.

Infuriatingly confident.

Exceedingly handsome.

Out-of-this-world sexy.

Yes, Dante Callaghan was all of those things.

But Aurora hadn't been interested in the notorious playboy when she'd first met him four years ago. And despite the way he'd managed to steal into her dreams on more than one occasion, she still wasn't interested. As far as she'd been concerned, Gio had been the man for her. Now she had to accept they weren't meant to be, but oh how she wished she didn't have to do it in George Jr.'s company.

"Refill, Ms. LeMonde?" he asked, shoving a champagne glass in her hands before she even had a chance to answer.

She took it, but no way in hell was she ever going to drink something George Jr. gave her.

He leered at her, his eyes barely making it above her neckline. Aurora was tall, and at 5'10" she had a perfect view of the pink half-dollar at the crown of George Jr.'s head.

Finally, his beady eyes made it up to her face. "You having a good time?"

What did he expect her to say? It was her company that was throwing the fundraiser, after all.

"Of course," she answered smoothly. "It's a wonderful event. Is your father here? I'd love to see him."

It was true. George Sr. was a trusted client. Honest, fair, and genuinely personable. How he'd ever spawned George Jr. was a complete mystery to Aurora. She peered down at the little man with a moment's worth of speculation.

He jumped at her momentary attention like a man trying to snatch a salmon out of the river with his bare hands. "He had other plans tonight, unfortunately. Have you given any more thought to my offer?"

Across the room, the woman at Gio's side threw her head back and laughed at something he whispered in her ear. Aurora's stomach tightened. Oh god. She'd never seen Gio whisper in someone's ear. Christ. Christ on a fucking cracker. Aurora felt herself spin away from time and place for a moment. It had been a good laugh too. Nothing put upon or manufactured about it. As much as she hated to admit it, Aurora was starting to think that in different circumstances she might actually like Gio's woman. That thought merely made her stomach clench even tighter.

Aurora tried to focus on George Jr.'s pinched little face. His eyes zipped up from her chest the second he realized she was looking at him again.

Aurora bit down her irritation. That kind of thing had been happening to her since she was about fifteen years old. In so many ways, men were a simple and predictable species. "I'm sorry, what were you saying, Mr. Mills?"

Something flared in George Jr.'s eyes when she referred to him so formally and it made Aurora want to puke. She never in a million years wanted to know what thought had put that lecherous look on his face.

"I was asking if you'd given my offer any more thought. You remember? I talked to you about it when we ran into one another on New Years? My beach house?"

Oh yes. The beach house. The little twerp had had the nerve to invite her, cold turkey, to a private weekend at his beach house in Malibu. Just the two of them.

"Funny," Aurora couldn't quite bite back the retort. "I thought that was more of a proposition than an offer."

George Jr.'s cheeks instantly went bright red. "I merely wanted to—"

"See if Ms. LeMonde could be enticed by your daddy's money?"

The deep voice came from behind her and so did the large, warm hand at the small of her back. Everything in Aurora's body tightened.

Great. Just what she needed right now.

Dante fucking Callaghan. She was so not in the mood for his oxygen sucking presence. Even so, she had to stop herself from instinctively turning around to admire how stunning he was sure to look. His light brown hair was short but somehow always looked a little bit messy and his sharp face was always shadowed and his blue eyes were always lit with an inner fire that made her feel warm when she stared into them too long. Dante wasn't loud or obnoxious, but he was enormous and commanding. Filling every room with his broad shoulders, all-seeing eyes, and constantly half-amused grin.

George Jr. sputtered and turned even redder than before. Dante was still standing just behind her, but she could practically feel his barely restrained amusement. She looked at her hands as one of his big paws plucked her untouched champagne away from her and replaced it with a fresh one.

Finally, he stepped in front of her, and Aurora was immediately swallowed up in the endless night sky of his deep blue eyes. Damn those gorgeous eyes. They just had to be attached to one of the most irritatingly sexy men in history.

"I was insinuating nothing of the sort, Aurora!" George Jr. insisted, puffing up like a balloon. "If you must know, Callaghan, I was simply—"

"Do yourself a favor and quit while you're ahead, Junior," Dante said, taking a casual sip of his drink and sliding even closer to Aurora.

Aurora barely stopped herself from choking on the

champagne she was swallowing. She'd always known that Dante was irreverent, but George Mills Jr. was the son of one of the most influential men in the city. As one of the best financial analysts in the business, Dante often teamed up with Gio on projects, which was the reason Aurora saw him so often.

Too often for her comfort.

George Jr., apparently choosing to retreat, at least for now, stiffly nodded in Aurora's general direction and turned on his heel.

Somehow she managed to bite back her smile of gratitude. "Honestly, Dante," Aurora said, looking at him admonishingly.

"What?" He raised his hands in an almost childlike gesture. "He was being a dick, so I made him feel like a dick. What's the harm in that?"

Aurora rolled her eyes and put a few more inches of space between them. "The harm is that he's the son of our biggest client."

Suddenly feeling as if she couldn't stand another minute of this—work obligations be damned—Aurora set her glass down and started to walk away.

"Oh, come on, LeMonde, you know that Mills isn't going anywhere, no matter how many times Junior gets his feelings hurt. He swears by you and Gio."

"That may be true," she retorted immediately, the words hot on her tongue and surprisingly easy to let loose. After what felt like a lifetime of repressing the things she wanted to say at the moment she wanted to say them, it was nice to be able to speak to someone with a little spice. "But what's the point in testing the theory? It's just like you to act without thinking and then disappear, no cares for the person who's going to have to clean up your mess!"

"What mess?" he demanded, getting in front of her and stopping her progress. "What person?"

Aurora pulled up short and longed to press her hands to her hips. But she knew exactly what that would look like. Two people fighting on the edge of a work party. As such, she folded her hands carefully in front of her and gritted her teeth into what she hoped would look like a polite smile to anyone watching from afar.

"George Jr.'s bruised little ego is the mess I'm referring to. And *I'm* going to be the one who has to nurse it back to health next time he comes by the office. All while desperately attempting to avoid his..." Hands? Eyes? Breath? Each option was equally abhorrent so Aurora gave up choosing. "Everything!"

Dante's jaw clenched before it relaxed and he sighed. "You're right," he said, cupping her elbow as she tried to step around him. "I shouldn't have butted in like that. I just wanted him to put his damn eyes back in his head where they belong."

"That makes two of us," Aurora conceded. She eyed him suspiciously. Why was he being so nice? So... human. Usually this far into an interaction he would have asked her out twice already. Instead, here he was, actually looking her in the eye and treating her like he understood her problems.

And then his eyes dropped to her breasts.

"He's lucky I didn't stitch his eyes closed for looking at you the way he was, Jessica."

Aurora's mouth dropped open. Aaand the asshole was back. Scanning her body with those deep blue eyes and calling her by the wrong name.

"Are you fucking kidding me, Callaghan?" Her professional veneer burned to a crisp as her temper spiked. She took a step forward into his space and planted a finger on his broad chest. Aurora was tall in her heels, pushing six feet, but he still towered over her. His sinful mouth quirked in a smile and his dark hair fell over his brow. "We work together for four years, you hitting on me like a frat boy the *entire* time, and now you can't even get my name right? Jesus. What am I, a magnet for fuck boys?"

She threw her hands up, as if asking that question of the cosmos itself, and Dante easily reached up, snatched her hand out of the air and laced his fingers through hers.

"I know your name, Aurora. Trust me. I've grunted it into my pillow enough times after business meetings with you."

Aurora schooled her face into a neutral expression, refusing to give him the satisfaction of her shock. "You're an absolute pig, Callaghan."

"No," he corrected, holding her hand tight when she tried to tug it free and tracing a circle on the inside of her wrist with his thumb. "I'm a man. And you're the most beautiful woman in the room no matter which room it is."

For a moment, his words caused pleasure to ripple

through her, but she reminded herself that's all they were: pretty words being uttered by a master of seduction. She smirked and tugged at her hand again. "Yet you can't seem to remember my name."

"I only called you Jessica because you look like Jessica Rabbit in this dress."

Aurora instantly regretted the surprised laughter that bubbled up out of her. She bit it back, ignoring the pleased look on his face. Aurora looked down at her red floor-length gown. It was pretty sexy, she supposed. But it was far classier than it was sex bomb. "I do not."

"You do too. Trust me, when I saw you from across the room my eyes did the cartoon *awooooga* thing." He used his hands to show his eyes bursting out of his head.

Aurora bit back another burst of laughter, crossed her arms and tucked her hands safely away from him. "Well. That sounds like your problem, not mine. Now, if you'll excuse me, I have clients to speak with."

She knew she was being snooty. And the Esposito Group *did* often partner with Dante's firm on larger projects, but honestly, if her behavior lost them the partnership, part of her would be relieved to not be around him as often. He was just so irritating. So big and direct. So frustratingly gorgeous and tempting, even if it was all a game to him.

Thankfully, she managed to walk away without Dante trying to stop her again. She told herself she wasn't disappointed. And in truth, she wasn't terribly surprised. Dante was a flirt, and he'd made it clear on more than one occasion how badly he wanted her, at least physically. But he never pushed too far. Moreover, he was always scrupulously professional in any meeting they had.

She didn't mind the attention he paid her. Just like she didn't mind his eyes on her ass as she strode away. She just couldn't give in to him—even when she was devastated by the knowledge that Gio was at this very moment with the redheaded woman of his dreams.

Aurora melted into the crowd and immediately let herself get sucked into a conversation. Ten more minutes and she was out of here.

With nothing but a weekend of eating ice cream and thinking about Gio. Oh joy.

She was just ducking away from the party, time obligations completely fulfilled, when a hand tapped her shoulder.

Aurora schooled her face into a friendly expression and turned right into Gio's chest.

"Leaving so soon?" he asked in a friendly way, no censure in his tone at all.

He looked happy, Aurora realized with both a sinking and a rising in her gut. She wanted him to be happy. She was just still reeling from the fact that he was happy with another woman.

"Headache," she said, knowing full well she was taking the coward's way out.

Gio's eyes instantly narrowed in concern. "Are you sick?"

"No, no," she hurried, feeling bad for lying. "Just a

little tired is all."

"Well, do you have it in you to make small talk for five more minutes? There's someone I've been wanting you to meet."

"Sure," Aurora said weakly, knowing full well who he wanted her to meet. Her chest tightened and her pulse kicked up like a storm off the water. She followed Gio in a daze through the crowd.

And then, there she was, the lovely redheaded woman. Standing right there. Looking perfect and petite and saying something to Aurora that she could barely hear over the roaring in her own ears.

Aurora shook hands, nodded her head, laughed politely in the right places. And then three minutes later she was drifting away from them, having said her goodnights.

She found herself in the back hallway toward the coat check, staring at a blank spot in the air. What the hell had just happened? She'd just met the woman that Gio was going to take home and make love to tonight. More than that, she'd just met Gio's future wife. She just knew it. She felt it in her bones. She was no psychic, not like her mother, but that didn't mean she didn't have above-average intuition.

Aurora felt a nauseous panic race through her. Gio's woman was so pretty. Sweet and kind. Rose. The prettiest flower there was.

"Aurora?"

She gritted her teeth at the gravelly voice that

instantly sent shivers down her spine.

"What?" she couldn't help herself from snapping as she turned and faced Dante in the dim light of the back hallway.

He raised his hands in surrender. "I didn't come back here to irritate you. Are you alright? You look like you've seen a ghost."

Aurora studied him in the bluish light, her blurry vision suddenly painfully clear. The noise of the party faded away as shadows cut across his face, accenting his sharp jaw, bottomless blue eyes, and dark brows. He was so big he damn near took up the entire hallway. He was so big, in fact, that he made Aurora feel small. Which was saying something, because she'd never been delicate or petite, even as a child.

The scent of him—soap and detergent and whiskey— drifted toward her in the small space and her pulse started racing. In that moment, for the first time ever, she willingly opened herself up to the attraction he made her feel and considered the possibilities…

She cocked her head to one side, studying him, and his brow furrowed like he was trying to figure out her mood.

A thought was uncurling inside her. A dangerous thought. But an interesting one nonetheless. Why should Gio be the only one getting busy tonight? She could damn well do with some good old fashioned sweaty sin. It had been long enough.

And maybe it would help. But only if it was hot. She

needed something hot enough to burn these feelings of jealousy and loss right out of her.

So, the question was whether or not Dante Callaghan would fumble in the end zone or if he'd give it to her right. Her eyes dropped to his large hands tucked halfway into his pants pockets. They moved to the confident width of his shoulders. And lastly, they focused on the noticeable bulge behind his zipper.

Her eyebrows raised. Well, even if he was terrible in bed, she could work with that. "Was it all talk?" she asked him, her voice husky and seductive even to her own ears.

He frowned and cocked a brow. "Excuse me?"

She took a step toward him. "All the pretty words you've had for me over the years. Was it talk? Were you ever going to do something about it?"

Dante's eyes immediately narrowed in comprehension while the rest of him remained perfectly still. "Are you asking me to do something about it?"

Aurora slowly shrugged one shoulder, feeling the fabric of her dress tighten around her breasts. She was feeling reckless and needy and like her soul might just dry up tonight if she didn't feed it something. And right now, what she wanted to feed it most was Dante Callaghan.

"For some reason, yes. I am. So what do you say?"

BOOKS BY VIRNA

KISS TALENT AGENCY
Book 1: Lip Action (Simon)
Book 2: Locking Lips (Caleb)

THE BEDDING THE BACHELORS
Book 1: Bedding The Wrong Brother (Rhys)
Book 2: Bedding The Bad Boy (Max)
Book 3: Bedding The Billionaire (Jamie)
Book 4: Bedding The Best Friend (Ryan)
Book 5: Bedding The Biker Next Door (Cole)
Book 6: Bedding The Bodyguard (Luke)
Book 7: Bedding The Best Man (Gabe)
Book 8: Bedding The Boss (Eric)
Book 9: Bedding The Baby Daddy (Dante)

HOME TO GREEN VALLEY
Book 1: What Love Can Do (Quinn)
Book 2: The Way Love Goes (Conor)
Book 3: I'm Gonna Love You (Brady)
Book 4: Best Of My Love (Riley)
Book 5: Because You Love Me (Sean)

HARD AS NAILS
Book 1: Hard Time (Street)
Book 2: Hard Case (Slate)
Book 3: Hard Core (Axel)
Book 4: Hard Place (Jericho)
Book 5: Hard Act (Davis)**

GOING DEEP
Book 1: Down Deep (Heath)
Book 2: Royally Deep (Kyle)

SAY YOU LOVE ME
Book 1: Say It Sexy
Book 2: Say It Sweet

ROCK CANDY
Book 1: Rock Strong
Book 2: Rock Dirty
Book 3: Rock Wild

PARA-OPS PARANORMAL ROMANTIC SUSPENSE
Book 1: Knox: Chosen by Blood
Book 2: Wraith: Chosen by Fate
Book 3: Dex: Chosen by Sin

**Coming Soon

ABOUT THE AUTHOR

Virna DePaul is a *New York Times* and *USA Today* bestselling author of steamy, suspenseful fiction. Whether it's vampires, a Para-Ops team, hot cops or swoon-worthy identical twin brothers, her stories center around complex individuals willing to overcome incredible odds for love. Bedding The Wrong Brother, which begins the Bedding The Bachelors Series, is a #1 Bestselling Contemporary Romance and a USA Today Bestseller.

Virna loves to hear from readers at www.virnadepaul.com.

CONTACT VIRNA HERE
Website: www.virnadepaul.com
Twitter: @virnadepaul
Email: virna@virnadepaul.com

www.ingramcontent.com/pod-product-compliance
Lightning Source LLC
Chambersburg PA
CBHW051429170626
46809CB00006B/2382